Stalked By A Demon

Lovers Of Lore, Volume 1

Stephanie R. Lowell

Published by Stephanie R. Lowell, 2025.

STALKED BY A DEMON

First edition. May 21, 2025.

ISBN: 979-8231001033

Written by Stephanie R. Lowell.

Also by Stephanie R. Lowell

Caught with a Lycan
Caught in a Lycan Favour
Caught in a Lycan's Protection
Caught Vamping Around With A Lycan
Caught Bewitching a Lycan

Love at first bite
The Vampire's Obsession

Lovers Of Lore
Stalked By A Demon
Fell For A Gorgon

The Moonstone Trilogy
The Druid Descendant
The Nephilim Rises
The Return Of Satan

Standalone

The Dimension to Destiny

Table of Contents

I would like to thank my mom for helping me edit most of my novels including this one and also for having enough faith in me to be my "PR" person (she didn't like the term book pimp).

Prologue

(Daemon)

The sky is a dark bluish grey like it is all the time, the ground is a red sand, both because of the lava not far below the ground and the blood of the battle that we didn't fare so well in. I live in Hell which may have a bad reputation, but really isn't so bad, in fact it has beautiful weather all year around. We are having a fight with Heaven which has been ongoing for millions of years if not more. The fight is about territory like every fight, they want more, we want more, and most importantly, neither of us wants the other one on theirs. It started off as a segregation between the angels and the demons.

The angels which are thought of to be beautiful and kind are just as devious as we are, but at least with us, it's expected. I wasn't always a soul sucking SOB, even though I was always a demon. A born one. I didn't always have the inherent need to suck souls, in fact I wanted to be an angel. When I was in my teens I talked to the angels about joining their ranks. They laughed at me and said they could never accept one like me. I didn't understand because I have never looked all that much different from them. The angels have a gold ring around the colour of their eyes that shines visibly brighter during strong emotions... mine are red. They have White wings with gold all throughout the feathers, mine are black with red. I found out I was never going to be an angel because I was born to be evil, at least that's what they told me and at that very young age, I believed them.

As the millennia have gone by I found those angels were right, I was evil. I found when I sucked a soul, I was stronger, more powerful.

The more vibrant the soul, the more power I had. If the soul was corrupt it was like a snack, it did the trick but left me needing more.

Every soul I stole proved I was the demon those angels said I was. Every soul also made me feel more desolate, the desolation increased until there was nothing inside of me but the desire to hunt, maim, torture and kill. I did all of the above to the angels who said I was nothing like them. I guess I proved they were right after all. One by one I watched them die in extreme and violent ways that were incredibly creative if I do say so myself.

I look at the battlefield and I must say my creativity is unmatched and has not diminished with time. Oh the amount of practice I have had at perfecting my technique, especially on angels and yet we battle here again today. They think they can stop us from creating our army, fear that one day we will win the war.

The thing about Heaven and Hell is that we both want to influence the human race. We want them to join our ranks and the only way to do that is to influence them into doing our bidding. To do the deeds that must be done. In my case, I make them do outrageous deeds like kill those they love. Do things that are so atrocious there is no redemption.

Not all souls go to heaven, or to hell. Most go to what is thought of as purgatory and it is anything but "nothingness" as it is viewed by mankind. It is beautiful by the standards of all creatures whether from Heaven or Hell and we are not allowed inside. We can however view it from the outside, none of us are welcomed.

The souls untouched by us go there and get the chance to be reincarnated over and over again. The humans we recruit are either weak of mind or strong in their desires. It usually doesn't take much persuasion to do the evil deed that will condemn them to hell. The souls that hold great goodness that I encounter and devour, they are the ones with the most strength. The ones that will help with my power the most. The most evil ones do help with my strength, it's not nearly as much as the good ones and the reason is unknown, and so the dark souls we make part of our army.

Thousands of years of this, fighting, claiming, strengthening and manipulating. With it comes thousands of years of maiming my enemies, losing and winning battles, but the truth is, we need more allies. We lost today, the bodies of my men are all around.

"Back to corrupt more souls?" A woman states from behind me. Not just any woman but my on again off again lover, my right hand woman, and my partner in crime, Gwendolyn. She's beautiful with long blond hair with a slight wave, same colour ring around her eyes as me and a body from any man's fantasy with curves in all the right places, flat stomach and legs that go on forever. She licks the blood from around her lips and smiles at me as she grabs me around the neck and flashes me to her bed room, sucking my tongue into her mouth and rubbing herself against me like a cat in heat. She moans before saying "Nothing turns me on like a good war, win or lose, I want you now".

My erection is painful in my pants as she releases it from the confines and strips herself bare. Foreplay is not her thing as she rushes for the main event, plundering herself on me. She is never soft, never gentle and with all the force we can muster we pound into each other trying to get release. She bites my neck and my nipples, but I mostly savour her lust for violence which is as strong as my own. Finally when we reach release she rolls off of me leaving me properly sated.

"So what are you going to do about what the seer said?" she asks after lying silent for a few minutes.

"I don't want to talk about this right now!" and I roll back on top of her, sucking and nipping at her skin, and rubbing my already recovered erection into her. She moans with more pleasure, but before I enter her again she says, "We need to discuss this now so we can save you from your own ruin".

I sigh into the base of her throat. "The girl and I won't meet for a few hundred years yet, and when we do, I'll slaughter her." We both laugh darkly before I add, "and her entire family."

"I can't wait, just the thought of a blood bath and mayhem makes me want to go another round." she says and we continue where we left off.

I AM OUT STALKING A potential target for our army. He is a belligerent drunk who enjoys to start fights in the local taverns. His name is Brandt and he has a mean streak a mile long but so far he just gets into fights, all I have to do is push him into murder. If I can get him to spill innocent blood, his ass is as good as mine so to speak.

I go over to the bar where he is sitting at and take the stool next to him. I see he is checking out the bar maiden. "She doesn't look like your type!" I say offhandedly.

He turns to me. "What the hell do you mean?"

I stir the drink in my hand that I ordered before approaching him nonchalantly. "I mean she is beautiful, clearly out of your league and would probably sleep with other men if you were together."

I hear a gasp. "She would not, she's too lovely for that!"

"Do you really think you could sate all her needs so she wouldn't stray?" He doesn't say anything right away. Minutes pass in silence.

"You could keep her for yourself though." I say hoping that he'll take the bait. Luckily he does.

"I'm listening."

"I wouldn't listen to this man." Another voice says from behind me. I turn and a see a tall man, with dark brown hair and bright green eyes. I than notice a gold ring around them, angel. "He will lead you to self-destruction. Just ask the girl on a date, she might say yes." and he walks away. Damn angel.

Chapter One

(Siren)

Another dollar, another day working at the flower shop. I have the natural ability to keep them looking beautiful and alive and because of this, I have become the most successful flower shop in town. I have lived here for the last two years and at first when I moved here, I had no idea what I was going to do. Residing here was not a choice that I personally made, I was forced into it. I was forced out of my home because I wouldn't marry a man that my parents preferred for me and he supposedly wanted me too. I did not want to be forced into a marriage I would not be happy in and that led me to being here where I am now, selling flowers.

Flowers remind me of a better time, my home was surrounded by their loveliness. The bushes were always the lushest of green and well taken care of, all the plant life strived around us. We all had the ability to keep them healthy and now I use that ability to sell that beauty to someone else.

I look around my shop and not one flower looks anything but vibrant, there is no wilting in my shop. My clientele always come back for more because they last weeks, sometimes months before even one flower dies.

It's the end of my shift so I am going to do what I always enjoy doing when I can manage to find the time. I leave my shop and walk to the forest just at the edge of town, not too far. I wander inside until I get to a clearing where I frequent. For me this is the most beautiful place I know, at least here. I walk to the edge of the river bank and sit on a log that I once dragged to the side so I could sit and enjoy the peace.

I close my eyes and I focus my energy on the water, the plants and the life around me and can feel the humming in my veins, almost a palpable thing. I feel the energy surging into my veins making me stronger. I look around and all the flowers are healthy looking and the grass is such a vibrant green it looks like it could have come from a fairy tale. Everything within one kilometre of me is renewed and rejuvenated.

Like all magic, mine is dependent on energy and plants are the epitome of energy because they are vastly accessible. The thing about magic is that, yes, I steal energy to replenish my own which one would think would end up killing everything around me. It's more like how a tree gives oxygen for one to breathe and then in return takes the carbon dioxide from all mammal's breath. With my magic I take the energy to be strong and powerful and in return, I give energy for the plants to feed off of. They are pretty much over dosing in euphoric rays of sunlight and rain without the actual substances. It's a big win/win.

Feeling refreshed I take off my shoes and most of my clothes, leaving me in only my bra and panties. I step into the water and once I get deep enough in, I dive into the cool depths. This is absolutely my favourite place in this town. It's really the one thing that keeps me here, this beauty that no one ventures to. A place I know I can be left alone to be the real me, without hiding from the world, pretending to be someone I'm not, and more importantly, something I'm not.

I close my eyes and revel in the feel of water, and bask in the rays of the sun, taking in all the energy around me. I can only go so long without feeding my magic before I weaken. I have decided since I first arrived here that I would fit in with the mortals around me. In order to do that I had to change my appearance. The world around me sees a young woman, with light blonde hair blue eyes, and sun kissed skin. This is not my true appearance, but that one probably wouldn't fit in here. It's not that I'm hideous or scary in my true form, it's just that, I would probably be seen as something that should be dissected or worse, vivisected.

It takes a certain amount of magic to maintain this body, so I have to come here as frequently as possible, but since it isn't always a possibility, it helps that I work in a flower shop. It might only be a small shop, but sometimes that's all I need, and other times it's better than nothing.

I get out of the water and sit back on the log in only my underwear waiting to dry off some. I know that when I leave here I will go back to my small lonely one bedroom apartment in a duplex where I will remain until I get up for work tomorrow. Because of my nature I refuse to create attachments to people that will inevitably become severed with time. I already lost everything and everyone I know and love and I refuse to feel that kind of pain ever again. The only way to avoid that is to never let anyone get too close.

I once had many friends and close family, and never thought that I would one day end up alone far, far away from home. I have been forbidden to return because of the pride of a man who wanted my hand in marriage and worse the pride of my family who decided that having me around was equivalent to having someone with Ebola in their company. As if my "dishonour" would spread rampantly and infect young and old if I wasn't exiled. Naturally they agreed to it. Not one of those people defended my honour, my right to choose and find love, they tossed me away like waste. Yet I have not only survived but thrived in a place foreign and incredibly frightening for those who are different. That's just normal everyday people, never mind someone of my calibre.

GREAT, SOMEONE IS MOVING into the apartment next door. The duplex I live in is a two story house cut in half so we both have two stories on either side. It's a pretty big house, originally built to have the two apartment's so both sides are incredibly spacious, which is good because I could never be cramped up. The place next door has been empty for a couple of weeks. The last people that lived there were a couple who were here before I was. They needed more space for a little one so they bought a house and moved on. As much as I enjoyed the silence it will be nice to have someone living in the empty space. I just hope whoever it is can keep things at a reasonable decibel.

I have a lovely patio that I love to sit at so I get a little snack and some fruit juice, freshly squeezed so to speak, for a person with magic. I go outside and sit on my deck to feel the fresh air blowing in my hair as it hangs loose down my back. I have a great lawn chair that can be put back like a bed so I lie in it where I can enjoy the fresh air. This is a nightly ritual when the weather permits and today is such a gorgeous day. It would be a shame to be anywhere but enjoying the outdoors. I wonder what my new neighbour would think of all that. Will I be seeing him or her outside on their deck? I sincerely hope not, at least while I am out here. I do not need someone to interrupt my "me time".

I LIE IN BED AND CAN here moaning from next door and a lot of pounding and oh my, someone really likes to praise the lord. Someone is clearly having a good time. Oh wow, I can hear the slapping of skin clear through the wall, the man is an animal. I grab my pillow and wrap it around my ears while trying block the erotic sounds.

After about twenty five minutes of it I decide to get up and watch some T.V. on the very loud magic box of bullshit as I like to call it. It's about two in the morning so there is nothing but infomercials on. If you want to buy something for hair removal or to grow excess hair, this is the hour you will find it. After flipping through the channels I find some old sitcom that hasn't aired since the 90's. Luckily for me it is still new.

(DAEMON)

What a night that was, hours and hours of the dirtiest raunchiest sex I have had in a... what's today? Thursday? Well then I guess since Monday. Man, those were the longest three days. What's-her-name was beautiful, sexy and lithe, and I loved how her body was so responsive. Too bad she was also a little psychotic, which is always the way with the women I take home. I told her it was time to get the hell out of my house... in of course the nicest way possible and she flipped her lid. She screamed and called me names so volatile, they made *me* blush. And why, oh, why do they always have to throw things, and always aiming for the face region? By the time I dragged her out of my house, yes, dragged her, I was all too happy to be rid of her. Worth it!

Ah, I lie in bed thinking about the job I have to do. All the souls I have to corrupt, the sex to be had, the people I must maim, and still I have time to relax in bed just like this. It's the alone time I really have to appreciate. After of course the corruption, the sex and the maiming.

I have to get my ass out of bed and get a jump on the day. All these delicious malicious deeds won't get done on their own. I go to my pants pocket and take out a crumpled piece of paper. I open it up and see all the names. Derek Anderson, Melissa McIntosh and Michael Bass. Those are the top three names on the list and first three people I get to seduce to the "dark side". Star Wars has nothing on the dark side to which I refer to. Melissa will be an easy one, no matter how difficult she tries to be. It's the other two that might be a little trickier. Well trickier for someone who doesn't have my experience. Sleep with a wife and that could lead to the best kind of calamity. A single guy can be talked into almost anything, especially when the desire to do something is already there. Talk him into seducing a girl and drugging her, maybe a little abuse, no problem. These people already want to do these things, I just put them on the right path, so to speak.

Maybe I'll start with Derek, he's a married guy, heavy drinker and loves to batter his wife. Broken bones are no stranger to her and neither is his debauchery. Hell, this guy's already has one foot in, well, Hell. I don't always get lucky enough that the dirty work can be done for me. This guy makes me look like a saint and I kill for fun, and this guy only aspires too. Today is going to be the day he kills his wife and I won't even have to be "the other man". Maybe I'll just sit at the bar and order him drink after drink and then what? Yes, got it. I will start a fight with him, it shouldn't take much, seems like the type of guys who is always right.

I have seen his wife before, she doesn't go out much, but I have my way of stalking my prey. You can see behind the sad eyes that she once was a beauty. I might not have to sleep with her but I can express my admiration for her. This is too easy. I might have to seduce an innocent afterwards just out of sheer boredom.

Next will be Michael, He's a drug dealer who has a penchant for lacing his drugs with a stronger much more addictive drug to have his clients come back for more. Talk some punks into ripping him off and BAM... literally.

Now Melissa, she is in love with her boss. Well love is not the unsavory word I would use. Obsessed on the other hand is right on the money, since I was watching her stalk him and his wife. I was also with her when she was cutting pictures of the couple and placing her own picture next to his. She will also be an overly unchallenging target.

THE DAY GOES BY RATHER uneventfully. A few blood baths, A little mayhem, but all in all a real disappointment. I was so bored with the whole ordeal I ended up running into a couple kids, one about thirteen and the other about seventeen and talked them into a little petty theft. You get to Hell like anywhere else... one step at a time.

Now I am with a lovely brunette with slightly tanned skin. Her name is Selina, or Serena... or Joan, something like that, by that I mean it was a female name. I bend her over the sofa and pound into her hard and fast. I need to let go of all this tension. I can feel my release is near so I grip her hips in a bruising grip and start to pound harder. Finally I feel the release I was seeking.

(SIREN)

I wake up yet again to yelling, this new neighbour needs to learn to shut up in the middle of the night. I hear him telling some girl to leave and her yelling at him about using her as some easy piece of ass. Well if the shoe fits honey, I mean girl, have some self-respect. I really hope it's not the same girl as last night. Finally hitting my bullshit threshold I say with all the power within, "Shut up and go home", and just like that the yelling stops and I hear the door slam. About time, now it's sleepy time. I lie back down and fall instantly back to sleep.

(DAEMON)

Another fight with a girl who wouldn't just get out of my house after I took my pleasure from her. She knew the deal before she came up here. I told her it was going to be quick and then she was out. Then as always there was the yelling and her acting like she didn't know what was going to happen. Weird thing though, she was yelling at me one minute than all of a sudden, she closed her trap and walked out.

I thought I felt a humming in the air, almost like an electrical current, one I have never felt before. It's not that it felt unpleasant, but nevertheless it made my hairs stand on end.

IT'S THREE THIRTY IN the morning and I'm on my way out the door. It's not true that there's no rest for the wicked, it's true that we seldom do. That means it's time to hit the club, an underground place demons like to hang out at, which usually means my top three favourite things, chaos, sex and maiming. Okay, so it's mostly two out of three of those things, maiming at this club is frowned upon although not forbidden. It's an exclusive club so if you start killing the members it really defeats the purpose. First of all, most of these souls are hell bound so 'when' they get there doesn't really matter. You see demons need to party too, eventually we'll have to 'downsize' and then enlist new clientele. It's the old "out with the old and in with the new" philosophy.

It's kind of a strip club, but there is a lot more than just stripping. There are private rooms, some BSDM play, though the term "play" is subjective. A lot of the people who come in here are higher class folk who don't want to deal with being ridiculed for their tastes which entail, but are not limited to sex play, cheating on a spouse, doing drugs in an environment where many drugs are being done and they are easily accessible and paying for a stripper to tease or to take into the private rooms. Others are crack whores who would do anything to get their next fix and know the clientele will give it to them. It really is a club for the most hedonistic of people who just do things that they feel will make them happy... though happiness itself isn't going to lead you to hell, many of the ways to achieve it will. That is what our club sells, or more specifically my club.

I opened it a few years ago because there is still a war going on between good and evil and although both are attracted to a good time, evil is addicted to it. It's open all night long, but closes about seven in the morning. Seriously, the wicked need to sleep sometime. The place looks like your typical club with dancers on the stage dressed in overly sparkly clothes. If you call it that since I have seen bathing suits showing less flesh. Hell, I have seen people completely naked showing less flesh. Maybe a bit of an exaggeration, but I make my point.

There is music playing loudly through the speakers and a huge dancefloor for everyone else to use. There is usually a lot of sex that happens out there for the exhibitionists and then you have the voyeurs who find that scene appealing as well. This club brings out all kinds and introduces them to each other, that's where the chaos comes in. Nothing like mischievous meeting mischievous and evil meeting evil. That's what makes it a party. Of course we get a lot of the partiers just looking for a good time on a Saturday night. Because of our exclusivity, that doesn't happen often and the ones who get through usually don't end up coming back. The ones who do are almost like a success story for me, to turn nice to naughty.

I look around and the party is in full swing. You would never know that most people would be waking up in a couple of hours to go to their boring old jobs where they will never know the fun they are missing out on.

So many mortals gyrating on the floor, alcohol induced at the very least. I see sweat dripping off brows, hair also slick, but nothing is slowing them down from the beat. The spell of the music is cast, the magic woven with no effort on our parts, all due to the tempo. I feel the beat taking me over, my toe wanting to tap but I resist. I didn't come here just to party, I have to check up on the place once in a while and make sure human life is valued in the club. What happens when they leave here is none of my concern. I would however prefer if they didn't kill our toys until everyone is done playing with them.

I walk around the club, the atmosphere never really changes, always charged with promiscuous promise that lures in the hedonistic and innocent looking for a good time. Anyone can be seduced, it just all depends on how far they are willing to go. It's not all about sex, no, it is about ripping down the walls that people erect after slithering through the crack. It's about feeling the Id in all of us, with nothing telling them it's a bad idea. It's about forgetting about the future, not thinking about those you love or who could be hurt by feeding yourself you're deepest desire. Desire is what keeps this club in business, it's what draws them all out here to drink without abandon and trust a stranger's touch. It's the crutch of the world I live in and the basis of how I pick my solders.

I can smell the lust in the air and it makes me want one of these mortal women. I wouldn't have to bring her home and worry about getting her the hell out. I see one and she is looking at me like a delicious meal. I crook my finger at her and she saunters on over. I point to the hallway leading to the private rooms and her smile widens at me. Game on.

The little vixen has a beautiful body but a soul so corrupt she will definitely have to be added to my army. After our time together in the room I really look into her soul and see her evil deeds. She is a lawyer which is almost bad all by itself, but she didn't get a head just by being good at her job, to which she is. No she used her womanly wilds and if that didn't work, manipulation and sheer cunning. She got some of the worse kinds of mortals back on the streets to reoffend over and over again and still she comes out and play. Sleeps well at night too.

It's not that she doesn't know the criminals she defends will do it again, she does, it's simply that she doesn't care, as long as she is the best in her profession. To her it's all about appearances, and she is most definitely seen as a viper, but is something much worse. She hasn't just won in court by being a great lawyer. No, she has paid off other criminals she defended to dispose of witnesses, and what they can't do, she does, like dispose of any evidence she can get her hands on. She is very good at being very bad.

She would be a great asset for our side. She is letting the vile back on the streets. She is getting them to do her dirty work for the most part and even seduces the ones who won't into being her little puppets. She is an evil genius which is a quality not usually within the fairer sex. I am going to have to get my men to keep an eye on this one.

Chapter Two

(Siren)

I had what felt like a long day at work. I didn't sleep well after my sleep was disturbed last night. The presumable male next door is a total pig if the last two nights are anything to go by, and to treat those women like that, I should curse him. Thank the heavens today wasn't a busy day or it would have been a right off for me.

A few people came in looking at flowers for an event. My favourite was a young boy who came in here looking for something for his sister because she had been crying at school. He didn't have any money but the tenderness in him melted my heart so I decided to give him any flower of his choosing for free. He chose one burgundy and white dahlia. "It's perfect!" he had said with a big toothy smile, I noticed he was missing one in the front.

Just as he was about to leave, his mother came barrelling in with panic written all over her face. "There you are!" she said as her shoulders sagged with relief. "You cannot just run off like that Tommy!" she chastised.

"I'm sorry mom, I had to get Ella a flower because she was sad." His mother's eyes softened and it looked like she wanted to cry.

"Sweetie, how did you buy these flowers?" she asked him.

"The nice woman said I could have it." He smiles back at me "Thanks!" he says as he takes his mother's hand.

His mother smiles at me, "It means a lot that you would do that." she says as she leads her son out of the store.

"It was my pleasure."

I look at the clock and realize it is time to close up. I lock the door and walk down a couple of blocks to the homeless shelter. A couple of times a week I try to volunteer there. It's so heart wrenching seeing mothers and children who have no place to go. It wasn't that long ago I was in there shoes and I remember how terrifying it was not having a safe haven.

I go to the kitchen and help the couple of people back there with cooking the daily meal. It isn't ever anything fancy, but to these people, any food is appreciated.

A mother comes in who can't be any older than twenty five and she has a small girl with her who is crying. "Momma, I want the pretty dress, why can't I have it"

"We can't afford it baby girl. Someday, hopefully I will be able to buy it for you."

I look at the girl and it breaks my heart to see a mother who wants to give her daughter the world but clearly can't even afford a decent meal. The look on the mothers face is completely stricken. This is the reason I come here. I walk over to the little family and sit next to the little girl. "Hi there, my name is Siren, and what is yours?"

The little girl gives me a watery smile "My name is Taylor." She sniffs back the tears, "I'm sad, I saw a pretty dress but momma says I can't have it". I look at her mother and see repressed tears in her eyes and then I smile at the little girl.

"What did it look like?" I ask her

"It was purple and puffy with lots and lots of sparkles"

"Wow, it sounds beautiful and I think I remember seeing a dress similar to that in the back. Just wait here okay?" I go to the back of the shelter and with my magic a dress materializes in my hands. I don't know if it's the exact same style but it fits the bill well enough. I go out to the little girl and hand over the dress.

"It's so pretty!" She looks at her mother, "Can I keep it... pleeease?"

Her mom smiles at her and when she looks back at me, I can see there is no way she would deny her child this one small gift. "Thank you, I don't know how I can repay you."

"No worries, it was my pleasure." I get up and walk back to the kitchen. I end up serving quite a few plates to men and women alike, and when I look around at them I see smiles on a lot of their faces. It's a miracle they can be so happy in such a dire situation.

"They look so happy out there." I say out loud to the middle aged woman next to me. I think her name is Doris.

"Yeah, they always seem to be the happiest when you are around. You always give off such an amazing energy, even I can feel it." Then she looks at the leftover food she is packing up to put away. "That was a really nice thing you did for that little girl. I don't know how you did it but it was a beautiful sight to see."

"It feels good to help the ones who need it most." I smile at her. "Well I'll wash up the dishes here and then I am going to go home and relax. I had a long night last night."

"Oh yeah, trouble sleeping?"

"The abominable man next door. He just moved in and although I haven't met him yet, I think I already dislike him"

"Oh a party animal is he?" she says with a little amusement.

"No, more like a man whore." I say shaking my head. "I really hope he can take a night off of his insatiable appetite before I end up knifing him." I say only half kidding. I don't think I will be able to be nice to this guy if this is going to be a regular routine. Me likes me beauty sleep.

I GET HOME AND AS USUAL I go out and sit on my deck, ready to enjoy a little peace. The sun is setting and there is a little bit of the night chill, but I don't mind.

"So you're my new neighbour." a very masculine voice says from beside me and I turn my head and glare at him. I have to admit he is a very good looking man... on the outside. He has shaggy blonde hair and brown eyes with what looks like red rimming the brown of his eyes. I can't tell for sure because of the dimming light.

"Well, it's nice to see the face of the man who has woken me up the last two nights." I seethe with distain.

"Hear anything you like?" he asks and he is clearly checking me out.

"Nope, not even a little!" this man actually disgusts me deep inside. There is something dark and primitive about him. Or maybe it's something worse.

"Well if you ever need a man between your legs, you can come here anytime."

"Yeah, apparently women coming over isn't the issue, it's just getting them to leave." Whoa, even I can hear my sneer.

"Yeah, what can I say, I'm good at what I do." He is so cocky it's walking the line somewhere between attractive and repulsive.

"Maybe you should consider taking them somewhere else? Like there house maybe? At least then they wouldn't destroy your belongings." and won't wake me up.

(DAEMON)

I was surprised to see my new neighbour out here on her deck at this time of the evening. She is a looker, I wouldn't mind getting her to come over tonight, the thought makes me want to lick my lips as my pants get a little tight. The thing that really draws my attention is her soul. It's so bright, a rainbow of colours, and many that aren't even part of the rainbow. Her soul would probably be quite the feast. This is a woman I am going devour in every meaning of the world. The fact that she seems to loath me makes me want her even more.

"Well I don't think I'll be having any guests tonight if you want to come over and give me a spin."

She laughs which surprises me before saying in a disgusted tone, "The only way that would ever happen is if you bound and gagged me, and even then I would find a way to flay you like a fish." Damn if that didn't turn me on more. The thought of her bound, delicious. The violence? It makes me absolutely giddy.

"Well if you ever change your mind..." and I tilt the beer in my hand in 'cheers'. She rolls her eyes but doesn't respond. I study her and I see she has long blond hair that is pin straight, even though it is tied back in a ponytail. She has big blue eyes but it's her soul that has me enthralled. I want that badly. I wonder what it would take for me to worm my way into her heart, or at least into her bed where I could take everything I want including her soul.

(SIREN)

I go back into the house where I feel thoroughly disgusted and a little bit dirty after my conversation with "horn dog" next door. I can't believe he hit on me, as if I would "tap" that. The man must live out his day looking for someone to screw and then his nights screwing them. I think I got syphilis just interacting with him. I better go wash up to make sure that shit doesn't spread.

I wake up in the middle of the night to the sound of fighting next door... Again.

I get up and throw on a housecoat, I am not going to let this slide again, no way. I march out the door and knock on his. He throws open the door in a fit of rage and then his eyes go wide with shock.

"Some people are sleeping, this is the third night you have woken me up and I'm done, SHUT UP!" I yell the last part because I am little miffed too.

"Why don't you mind your own God damn business you stupid bitch?" the woman says.

"Wow that's pretty ballsy for someone who is getting all but thrown out of this man's house and putting up quite the fight about it. I mean have some self-respect." The woman glares at me. I turn back to what's-his-face-oh-yeah-I-don't-care and say, next time you wake me up, I might not be so nice. I look at the girl again "As for you, get lost." and just like that, the woman walks out, shouldering me on the way by.

"Why thank you!" The sonofabitch says.

I give him a look I'm sure would have disfigured a lesser man. "I. DID. NOT. DO. THAT. FOR. YOU!" And I turn around and scurry back home.

I GO TO WORK, COME home and all the while I feel like someone is watching me. I feel this malevolent energy that raised my hairs. It was one thing when I felt it at work but now I'm home on my own domain and I still feel it. I look around, but there is nothing out of place, nothing out of the ordinary.

I look out the window, in the closets and under furniture, but still there is nothing that would give off such a strong energy. I finally sit on the couch when I suddenly get this weird feeling on the back of my neck, like puffs of air.

(DAEMON)

I followed her all day long in the spiritual realm, "ghosting" as I call it. The new age term is just as impressive when considering one's ability to just vanish.

I watched her at her flower shop, and watched how she dealt with her customers. Ever since last night I couldn't disregard this beautiful woman who could get a woman out of my apartment simply by demanding it. I sit next to her on the couch and get close enough to breathe her in, she smells like happiness, if happiness had a scent.

She flips through the channels on the television and stops on a cartoon with faeries. Her face lights up and she sits back enthralled by the movie. She gets up and makes herself some popcorn and then sits back down. Half way through she starts yelling "BOO! That is inaccurate, faeries don't act like that!" and she starts throwing popcorn at the screen. "Do your research." Weird that she would get that worked up over a cartoon with mythical creatures.

I watch the cartoon, peering over at her frequently and watching her reactions until I stopped watching the cartoon and put all my focus on her. She would smile when the little faeries would fly and sometimes she laughed at their antics. All of a sudden she starts yelling, "Don't marry the faery prince, your future will be dictated for you. Well.... it might be anyway." she mumbles the last part.

Finally it's the end of the movie and it's one of those sappy happily ever after's (gag) and I see a tear stream down her face. Instinctually (which is weird because it goes against all of my instincts) I swipe away a tear with my thumb ever so lightly. The moment it touches my skin there is a burning yet freezing feeling that goes through my body and makes me feel warm inside, almost at peace. I instantly wipe the tear on my pants, regretting even touching the foreign creature who happens to be my neighbour. When I look back at her she is lightly rubbing her cheek.

I decide I have to go out and start a fight somewhere. I have to eradicate this feeling inside me. About fifteen minutes later I make it to a biker bar where the local wannabe biker gang meet up. No one is more fun to fight with then someone who constantly thinks they have to prove 'how tough' they are. I walk past a group of them standing near the pool table and shoulder bump one of them on my way past. After the guy steadies himself he yells "You better watch yourself."

"Or else what? You'll shoot me?" I continue on and order a beer. Just as I take my first swig he knocks the beer out of my hand. I look up at the guy "You owe me a beer." and I know things are about to get interesting.

"Yeah, that's the thing, you walk in to OUR bar and start shit." before I know it (or so he thinks because I anticipated this outcome to begin with) he punches me in the nose. I hear the cartilage crunch and feel the blood gush. I look up at the guy with a grin on my face and start punching him back. There are a lot of fists flying. I feel his face under my fists repeatedly and it inspires me to hit him harder. His friends jump in (always being the tough guys by outnumbering their target) and I see a fist flying at me from the side. I duck my head and he ends up hitting one of his companions.

I know there is going to be a knife, and then the fun really begins. Oh there it is. I see the sliver glint in the light before it goes into my side. I look down at the knife. "Thanks for the knife but you didn't have to." I pull it out of my side. The look of horror on the man's face who stabbed me only lasted a moment before I swipe out and slit his throat. Then in a flash I pull my arm down and back and stab the guy behind me. The other guys put up their hands in defeat. One of those guys was the one who hit my beer out of my hands. I throw the knife and it goes right into his throat. I sigh "Now I'm done." With that I turn around and walk out of the bar.

The fight wasn't quite the rush I was hoping for but it did obliterate that warm happy feeling inside. I shiver just thinking about the horror of it. Next thing you know I'll be cuddling little woodland creatures. That would be a nightmare.

(SIREN)

Even though it's late at night, I can't sleep and since I enjoy sitting on my deck, I go out there to relax. Unfortunately it looks like my neighbour had the same idea.

"Can't sleep?" he asks.

"No which is too bad really because for once it's quiet." Is that agitation in my tone? Yep, it most certainly is.

"Testy, testy." He says with disapproval. "Maybe I could do something to relax you." he adds suggestively.

"Thanks but you have done enough as it is." I get up to go back inside. "I suddenly realize it wasn't air I needed after all."

THE NEXT NIGHT I DECIDED after a long day at work and since I haven't gotten out much since I moved here, I would go to the club in town. It's really the only one, to the point that people just call it 'the club'. I think the name of it is something erotic or blood thirsty, either way it's naughty. I decide to leave my long blonde hair down and put on a black leather dress that goes to my thigh with a V neckline. The perfect addition is leather knee high boots. Damn I look good if I do say so myself.

I get to the club and everyone seems to be having a good time. I go to the bar and order a shot. I don't need to drink much because my magic is intoxicating enough, but a drink here and there can be fun. After I take a shot I go and dance on the floor and before I know it, I have some guy grinding with me. I let him have his fun for a few songs before I get hot and decide to sit down at the bar where I order another shot.

A catchy tune comes on and I get up and start dancing again. I feel so free, and sexy, a feeling I haven't felt in a long time. Every time I am dancing alone, it doesn't last long. After quite a few songs I get over heated and decide to go out back to cool off. I notice someone following me on the way out, but I don't think much about it until he pins me to a wall down a narrow exit where no one would hear me scream.

Feigning nonchalance I ask, "What do you think you're doing?"

He starts to feel me up, "What does it look like sexy. I saw you dancing out there and decided I wanted you for myself."

"Now that wasn't very smart." I smile up at him, the kind of smile that says "something very bad is about to happen". When I look into his eyes, I see they are royal blue with a red ring around them. I reach into his chest and pull out his still beating heart and hold it in my hands. He backs away from me pretty quickly for a man without a heart. I close my eyes and force out a tear and let it drip onto his heart before walking over to him and forcing it back into his chest.

He falls onto his knees in obvious agony. "What did you do to me?" he whines.

"I poisoned you. The thing I love about the heart is it beats blood and poison through the rest of the body. You are going to feel a lot of irrevocable pain. Things like guilt, remorse and my favorites, compassion and empathy." I giggle at the look of horror on his face. "The perfect recipe for self-loathing don't you think?" A couple of other people who I suppose also needed air, witnessed what happened and when I turn to walk back into the club (because I need a drink more than fresh air) they scramble out of the way.

"Anyone want to dance?" I ask them and I hear one of them announce, "We should do it, she took *him* down," and they quickly follow suit. Well the guy I poisoned just kind of leaned against the wall murmuring something about how I ruined his life and blah blah blah.

After dancing with the fear struck men for many songs, I feel someone grab my shoulder with a firm grip and turn me around. Now I'm face to face with the man I want to torture more than anyone.

(Daemon)

I was flirting with a beautiful redhead when I saw a very attractive woman with a lot of male attention. She was bumping and grinding with some of the scariest men that come to my club. When she turned around so I could see her face, I see it's my neighbour and I feel my heart speed up.

I stroll over to dance with her when one of the men stops me with a hand to my chest. "You don't want to get involved with that one." I push him to the side. "Seriously, she'll rip your heart out like she did to Angus." Angus is a very big, very scary demon who doesn't take any woman seriously. I doubt this little girl could do too much to him.

"I am the heartbreaker. Now move!"

"No, she literally ripped his heart out and now he's blubbering like a baby over in the corner." I look over, but I can't see him through the crowd. I push the brick wall of a man out of my way and walk over to the woman I can't seem to stop thinking about. "It's your heart," I hear behind me. I turn her around and when she sees it's me who has approached her, her eyes go wide before they narrow.

"Back off." a man who has been dancing with her snaps.

"She's my neighbour." I tell him before I turn back to her, but she looks none too impressed.

"Why are you here?" her tone clearly agitated.

"I thought I would find some prey here so I wouldn't have to take them home and wake up the sweet little girl next door."

"No, I mean what are you doing over here, talking to me?" She backs away from me. "Maybe tonight I'll be keeping you awake." She smiles wide and turns away to dance some more. There is no way she will be bringing anyone home, not that I care or anything.

She grabs a man by the hand and drags him away to dance, and she grinds against him in an erotic dance. A vicious emotion hits me and I want to kill the piece of shit she's dancing with. She wraps her arms around his neck and he looks like he is enraptured. Rage unlike any I have ever felt before takes over and I go over to her and rip her away from the demon male she was all but screwing on the dance floor.

"If you don't get out of my way, I will make you and trust me when I say that you won't like my methods." I can tell that's not a threat on her part and that she will most definitely follow through on it. For some reason I don't care, I don't understand this darker than usual emotion I feel, but she will not be dancing with these males anymore if I have anything to say about it. As one of the most powerful demons in creation I have plenty to say about it.

"Go find yourself a nice woman to corrupt." Her tone has so much venom that it take me aback.

"Maybe I don't want any other women tonight." To that she laughs hard, but there is an edge to it.

"I'm sure." She sobers, walks over to me and goes on her tip toes to look into my eyes. She is so close I can smell her, feel her breath wisp across my face. "If you do not leave me now, I will stab you in the heart without a seconds thought." and the malice is palpable. "I despise everything about you and would love nothing more than a reason to do so." She turns away and grabs her partners hand and continues her dance. I turn away from her, disbelieving what just happened. I will go for now, but I will watch her every move.

(Siren)

After an incredibly fun night despite that impossible man, or maybe partly because of him, I head out into the night to make my way back home.

I am enjoying the silence of the night when I hear something in a dark alley. It sounds like someone struggling when I hear a hiss of pain and smell the metallic scent of blood. I rush into the ally to see a woman in her twenties leaning against a building, holding her stomach as blood seeps through her fingers. "Hey you!" I yell at the man with the knife. "Want to pick on someone your own size now?"

He looks me up and down with a smile that says 'you'll be plenty fun to play with'. We shall see.

"Are you sure you are prepared to play with the big boys?" He laughs.

"Big boys eh? Big boys don't play knifey stabbey with innocent little women." Quicker than I would have thought possible for this 'big boy', he brings his arm with the knife up and toward my face. I clap my hands on either side of the blade and stop its progression and knee him in the junk. He lets go of the knife and I wrap one hand around the blade until I feel the sting of it. Then I slip the knife into the other hand by the handle and approach the now kneeling man.

He looks up at me with the knife and stands up in spite of the pain. He pounces toward me with his fist out to punch me. With my bloodied hand, I grab his wrist as I move my head out of the way. He screams in agonising pain but nothing compared to how he will be in a moment. I push his arm aside and put my bloodied hand on his face and he falls back to his knees.

"OUCH, what are you doing to me?" The thing about me is everything about me is magical and can be used as a weapon or a treasure. My blood is like acid to exposed human skin. I can feel his face melting under my hand. I am about to stab him when I hear the whimper of the girl he stabbed. I turn away from him and go to her side.

I look her over and see that her wound is fatal and she will bleed out if I don't do something, and fast. I rest my uncut hand over top of her wound and use my magic to heal her. Not completely though, because that would be suspicious for these humans, but just enough that she won't die, or at least not immediately. She will need a hospital.

I grab the girl's cell phone and call 911, knowing the man who did this is on his way to seek help for himself and that he will not likely return. With that knowledge I feel better about leaving her alone in the night waiting for help to arrive. I cannot stay here for I need to remain inconspicuous to live amongst these people.

Chapter Three

(Ezekiel)

I have kept my eyes on Daemon for more centuries than I would like to count. I have intervened in many of the corrupted souls he seeks to recruit as part of his army. I have been too late just as often and have watched as the souls self-destruct with the knowledge that I'm unable to do anything to save them. All the while knowing another angel or myself will one day be the cause of their death absolutely. I have watched him not only destroy souls but also devour them.

I cannot always be around to protect the mortals from all evil as I have my own wars to wage, my own army to create and can't be everywhere at once.

I watched his intrigue in this woman who lives next door to him, she is both beautiful and merciless. I know he stalks her and watches her, hoping to prey on her. I am not sure what she is, whether she is good or evil, but after the vile acts that she has sowed, I'm leaning toward evil. If so she must die.

I watched her destroy the demon at the club, saw that even hours later he was still sobbing and pulling at his chest as if he was willing himself to rip out his own heart. I watched as she tortured a criminal with... her blood? She then did the inconceivable and helped the man's victim before she could die, saving her life. The whole situation was so surreal it was like being in some twilight zone. She could be as evil as a demon at times and as good as an angel at others. What is she?

I can see that Daemon is pondering the same thing as he watches her in the alley. He followed her in the spiritual realm, as did I, and I can see the shock on his face and the wariness her actions have created. I can see him, but he cannot see me for I am in the shadows on the other side of the street.

This woman who seems to be able to bring total destruction or salvation needs to be either put in her place or obliterated. I think I might need to do my homework on her, up close and personal.

(SIREN)

Another day at the flower shop goes by uneventfully when a beautiful man walks in to buy flowers for his mother. His hair is a dark brown, his eyes an emerald green with a gold ring. And his smile? To die for.

After chatting and flirting and exchanging names to which his he told me his was Zeek, he asks, "Would you like to go out for dinner with me tonight?"

"I'm sorry I have plans." They may involve seducing and maiming a man who stabbed an innocent last night, and because he has my blood in his system he will be easily tracked.

"What's the worst that could happen from one date?" I don't know, a second and third? I don't say that though.

"I really am busy tonight, maybe tomorrow night instead?" At first with the rejection his smile wanes only to grow wider when I concede.

"Great, well until tomorrow." He walks out, without the flowers he came in to get. There is something very unusual about this situation.

THE FOLLOWING DAY, I leave the store and follow the 'leash' to my victim, but before I confront him I change my identity. I morph into a woman with short brown hair and eyes similar to the woman he stabbed. I give myself more curves and heft and then make my way to his front door. I ring the doorbell and after a short wait he answers. I slightly flinch at his distorted face externally, while feeling great satisfaction internally.

"What the hell do you want?" he asks none too kindly.

"Sorry to bother you, but I was visiting my friend with my kitten and she seems to have gotten loose. I was wondering if you have seen her anywhere." I state as sugar sweet as possible. "A neighbour said he saw her wonder over here."

"Nope, I haven't seen any kittens." he replies and he seems to be about to say something else when he looks me up and down. "Would you like to go out back and look for yourself?" I smile innocently and nod, happy he took the bait.

Once in the back yard I start looking around to see all the nook and crannies my imaginary kitten could have hidden. I look at the tops of trees first and then bend to look under his back steps. He just watches me but doesn't help.

Suddenly he is right behind me and I know he is about to do something that will earn him the death sentence I have come to deliver. He pulls my backside against his front and moans. "You know that no one can see us right now." He starts to grind against me. "Just because my face is destroyed doesn't mean my manhood is." His grip on my hips tightens.

"I don't think so." I pull away from him. "You are not my, uh, type." I add with disgust, more to taunt him than anything.

"You bitches are all the same." He grabs an axe I did not see sitting next to the steps. He goes to swing it at me when I stop it mid-air with magic before I laugh coldly.

"Really? You thought you could kill me?" Then I change my features back to the one he would likely never forget and his eyes widen in terror. "Have you learned nothing about harming innocent little women?" I take his knife out of the waistband of my pants, still with my blood on it and I stab him with it and twist the knife for good measure. He falls on to his knees "Well... isn't this a familiar sight?" I push him down with my foot against his chest, pushing the knife in further. "Well thanks for the help and the offer, but I think I'll have to decline, but tell me if you see my precious kitten." With that I walk away from him. I turn my features back to the brunette just in case anyone saw me wander back here.

AFTER A QUICK SHOWER, I dress casually in a pair of jeans and a pale pink short sleeved shirt and I tie my hair back in a ponytail. I head out to the soup kitchen because killing leaves me with a need for redemption. That truly isn't the reason why I started going to the soup kitchen though. I like the feeling I get when I make someone smile and know I made a difference in their life. Sometimes making a difference in one person's life means ending another's, and though I do enjoy reaping out punishment, it leaves me needing to do something that brings a better life.

I walk into the soup kitchen and a few of the homeless smile and say a greeting. I go to the back of the kitchen to help cook when I get a prickling sensation of being watched. I look around, but the only people I see are too busy cooking and cleaning dishes to be watching me.

After the cooking is done and I am feeding the ones who didn't get anything earlier before I arrived, I hear a little voice. "I was hoping to see you here." I look over and see a little girl wearing a very beautiful dress that I gave to her, but nothing is as beautiful as the smile on her pudgy little face.

Seeing how happy she is makes me smile wide. "You are so beautiful in that dress." I look over at her mother who is watching her daughter with a happy smile.

(Ezekiel)

I watch this anomaly of a woman as she... helps the homeless? After watching her with the man from last night, when she came here I thought she was about to kill the homeless, because they clearly haven't suffered enough. But no, she volunteers her time here.

I see the cutest little girl walk over to her in a dress so sparkly and frilly that any little girl would be jealous of it. She goes up to Siren (I found out her name earlier at the flower shop when I asked her out) and thanks her for the dress. The smile of delight on Siren's face would make a weaker man weep. She truly is the most beautiful woman I have encountered who isn't angelic.

Siren holds her hands behind her back and something appears there, and I have the sudden urge to pounce on her before she can harm the girl. Instead of something menacing, I see a doll appear. She takes it from behind her back and hands it to the girl. "I got this for you."

The little girl's whole face lights up. "Thank you so much." Her mother is so thankful that she says, "You have really done so much for her and I will never be able to pay you back".

To that Siren smiles. "Her happiness and gratitude is payment enough." She is about to walk back into the kitchen when a man stops her by her arm. He is smiling up at her and she smiles back at him, such a warm smile.

"You just made that little girls day, and probably her mother's too." There is such warmth and awe in his tone.

"Knowing that makes the bad things that happened today worth it." When she says that, I wonder if she is referring to the man she slaughtered with little or no remorse. Seeing the other side of her makes everything about her more confusing. I have never seen anything kill so viciously and without mercy only to come to a place to help people and put smiles on their faces without getting anything in return. I am baffled by it. It makes me want to know her better, and maybe I will when I go on that date with her. Maybe I will get more dates to find out what is needed to be done about her.

(Daemon)

What the hell is she?

I saw her kill last night without mercy which just turned me on and made me want her more. It also shocked me that she did it without a single weapon. She used her blood and it burned that man, a man I had coerced into taking that woman out back into the alley. I did not see the rest of that scenario happening though. She clearly has some ability beyond my comprehension. Far beyond anything I have ever seen before. She was so gorgeous last night too, even more so after that murder today. How I want to knock on her door in the middle of the night and beg her to let me into her bed. Unfortunately she made her feelings toward me very clear.

"Hey man." One of my demon consorts greet me. "That was a crazy night last night wasn't it? And that minx, whew, did I want to get my claws into her. Did you hear what she did to Angus? The guy was acting like fragile little girl..."

"Shut up! I don't want to talk about her!" I do want to stab you in the throat for talking about her though. "How did the debauchery go with those desperate men?"

He laughs. "They will definitely be joining us sooner rather than later. It isn't hard to convince a bunch of depraved men to do horrible things in the name of vengeance. Especially when you tell them all the pros and none of the cons."

"You are one sneaky sonofabitch which makes you so damn good at your job."

"That's why I'm your right hand man right?"

I glare at him, he knows he isn't my right hand man by choice, but while Gwendolyn has been avoiding me for the past two hundred years, he stepped up and took her place... for now.

(SIREN)

I finally make it home and check my mailbox and there is a letter for who I assume is my neighbour. Funny how all the times he has harassed me, I never got his name. Huh, Daemon, that's weird. I knock on his door and am surprised to see he is there.

"Oh look who finally came a knocking." He sounds way too amused.

"I got some of your mail." I hand it over to him. "Demon? That's your name?"

"Yeah, but I pronounce it Damon. Your name is Siren?" At my quirked eyebrow he says, "I may have checked inside your mailbox. Isn't that like a demon?"

"Touché, but they only lure sailors and devour them because sailors are attracted to their voices. They would hunt them and capture them. Like for like"

"Huh, facts about mythical creatures." He rolls his eyes.

"Just because you have never seen them doesn't mean they don't exist. I have yet to meet a demon." and with that I walk away.

"Good point." I hear him mutter quietly.

I GO INTO THE HOUSE and I instantly get a feeling inside from a familiar magic that could only be that of my sister Cassandra. I walk into the room and see a note on the bedside table. I look at the familiar script and then rip the envelope open to peer inside.

Emergency- Your ex fiancé has decided that he wants to find you, I don't know why but be prepared.

There was no greeting, no sign off, just the warning, one which I must take seriously. She wouldn't have sent me a letter like this if she wasn't concerned, which is so unlike her. I feel a foreboding that I am unfamiliar with, and close my eyes to take a deep breath. I can deal with this.

I sit down in my living room and flip on the television. I don't know how long I have been staring at the screen with no recollection of what is on it when a familiar sound interrupts my thoughts with a start. Yep, the familiar moaning of whoever the neighbour has decided to 'bless' today. To think he invited me to be his companion. I laugh a little to myself. Yeah like that would happen. He doesn't even know where he has been and I'm allergic to herpes, nasty rash it is. Seriously, would one celibate day really kill the man? It's not like he cares one iota about any of these women, which this one will surly find out right after he is done with her and kicks her out like all the others. I roll my eyes at the thought. Why do they let themselves be used and discarded and then want more? Some things in this realm I will never understand.

I look at the note from my sister and remember the man who was my best friend. We grew up with each other. We laughed, played, and even fought with each other. I trusted him until it all came to an abysmal end. His betrayal cut deep and proved just how little he thought of me. To be used like that? I will never let it happen again. To think he wants to find me. Well, I guess I am going to have to come up with a plan to destroy him. Daemon is always a stark reminder of the man in my own past, and those women, always so desperate for his abuse.

I walk over to the patio door and catch my reflection in the glass. Another thing he took from me, my identity. I twist my blonde hair around my finger, but it's all wrong. This is not what I look like. The pale skin, though is similar, has too much pink undertones. My eyes are the only thing I didn't think would freak out the humans.

Sometimes, for brief moments, I look as I truly am, but I always fear someone will catch me.

I sigh and open the door and sit outside, trying to escape the negative thoughts of my life altering past, there is nothing I can do about it now.

I hear someone coming up the street sobbing, the sound masculine. I get up and peek around the side of my house to the front of my street and see the man who thought he could have his way with me last night. The one who now has his heart poisoned. I go to the door and peek through the window as he goes up to Daemons door. Who is this guy and how does he know him? Daemon is not going to enjoy being interrupted, again I smile coldly. This is about to get interesting. Maybe I should make some popcorn. Maybe I should make things a little more interesting and go out there. I wonder how well that would go.

"What the hell do you want?" I hear Daemon sneer.

"S-s-something is w-wrong with m-me. I-I can't s-stop cry-ying."

"That isn't my problem, now go."

"H-how can I f-fix this?"

"Um how about by not being a whiney baby and grow a pair." I hear the door slam.

I open my door. "Maybe I might know what your problem is." He looks at me with so much fear in his eyes I smile and give him a little wave by wiggling my fingers. He backs away with sweat dripping off his brow but on the bright side, he stopped crying. That's a bonus right? Unfortunately, in stepping away from me, he fell down the steps off the front porch.

Daemon chose that moment to open the door, kicking the girl out and then he stops and looks at his friend, than at me. "What?" I grin. "I think I scared him." I say in the most innocent tone I have. To which he rolls his eyes and tells his bud to come inside.

I AM GETTING READY for that date with Mr. Tall, dark and sexy. I don't know what to wear so I put on a short sleeved pink blouse and jeans. It goes well with my current complexion. I get to the restaurant and sit down. It looks like I beat him here. I am not waiting long when the man who could take your breath away spots me and gives me a smile that could melt the arctic.

"Sorry I'm a little late." He sits down across from me. "I had a little business I had to catch up on."

"No worries, I hadn't been waiting long." I look at him with his dark brown hair, his weird green gold eyes and teeth so straight and white that he could have just walked off a runway. To be honest, I don't keep up with tabloids and all that stuff, so for all I know he did.

After ordering our food and drinks he smiles at me. "So how long have you lived around here?"

"For a couple of years." I smile at him. "And yourself?"

"Well I have only been here for a couple of weeks. I need to do a job here. I come here from time to time to check on things."

"Well what kind of work do you do?" Maybe he is a model.

"My job is extremely boring. Let's talk about you. What made you move here?"

I debate my answer, but I might as well just stick to the truth. "I was disowned by my family and this town seemed as good as any. I appreciate all the wild life and landscape." He doesn't need to know the "whys".

"Disowned? I can't imagine a girl like you would do anything bad enough to warrant that."

Well luckily he doesn't know my family. "Sometimes it's a matter of a disagreement." He raises an eyebrow at me. "This is not a first date conversation." I tell him with a tone that is lighter than I feel.

"Okay, fair enough. What made you want to work at a flower shop?"

To that I give a bit of a giggle, "I like pretty things." The reason again is none of his business. "There is something about being around flowers that manages to make me feel better." Not a lie.

"Well I must say, your flowers are very pretty." Again he has his play boy smile. This man only needs to smile and I'm pretty sure at this point he could ask me to chew off my own legs and I would think it was the best idea I ever heard. I need to chill out.

"I think I might recall seeing you at the club the other night. Looked like some guys might have been giving you a hard time." I know at that my face darkens for a second. I hope he couldn't read anything from that moment of him catching me off guard.

"I dealt with it and that's all that matters." I try to sound as nonchalantly as possible.

"At least it didn't stop you from enjoying yourself." The way he says it almost seemed to have an undertone of accusation or something but I could be imagining it.

"Can't let one asshole stop the party right?" I take a sip of the wine he ordered. I really hope this doesn't end up as an inquisition because I think his head looks really nice attached to his neck.

"So Zeek, what brought you to the night life?" hoping to change the subject.

"Just looking to have a good time like everyone else there." He smiles as if he knows how disarming it is.

We end up chatting and eating the rest of our meal. It isn't long before we are paying our bill and walking out the door.

Chapter Four

(Daemon)

I let Angus stay overnight while he sobbed like a little bitch the entire time. I was hoping he would fall asleep and then I could put him out of my misery. I don't know what happened to this monster of a demon, but I think death might be doing him favour as well. The way he looked at Siren with such inconceivable terror made me want to laugh out loud. How a beautiful little girl who yes, happens to have obvious powers, could manage to destroy a seasoned evil like Angus is beyond me.

He cried all night and most of the day, I'll admit he might have stopped when I came out with my blade and told him I was going to cut off his head if he didn't shut up for a few hours. Surprisingly he valued his life enough to do so, though I might cut off his head anyway.

Siren left hours ago dressed delectably and by that I mean deliciously. I wanted to follow her to see where she was going looking like that, but decided I couldn't leave Angus to his own devices. Who knows what he would do if he was left alone. I'm more afraid he will go out cuddling kittens and singing to birds than anything else at this point. He claims that the 'neighbour bitch' ripped out his heart and poisoned it. Although I saw her destroy a man in the alley, that man was a mortal human who was easily destructible. If she did do this to one of my best men, what else is she capable of? I still can't figure out what she is. Her soul is so beautiful that after I get her into my bed, devouring her soul is going to be the best treat I have had in my existence to date.

All that power that she has, all that light, it will be like the best kind of gourmet buffet, all in one sexy little woman. I have to find a way to get past this loathing she has towards me. I have to get her to trust me somehow so I can have all of her.

I look over at the sad excuse for a demon that is sitting on my couch staring blankly at the floor. Thank god he shut the hell up finally. "So you want to go to the club and find you a nice woman you can bury all your troubles in?"

He looks at me but instead of his usual cold and callous smirk there is nothing. He just shakes his head and then continued to stare at the floor. I am going to have to cut off his head if he doesn't snap out of it. What will my enemies think if I not only have this sniveling demon man-child on my team but actually allowed him to live? I would become a laughing stock. No that is not allowed.

"Angus you better pull your head out of your ass very soon or that threat I made earlier is going to be a very promising reality." and I storm out the door to find me a woman to lay and a soul to feed on.

I DON'T GENERALLY FIND the souls I need to feed on at the club. Those souls are already corrupt and I need one that is a little more pure. I walk by a dance studio and there she is. She is tall and slender with long dark brown hair and dark brown eyes. Her skin has a pleasant tan and her soul looks absolutely delicious. I lounge outside of the studio and wait for her to leave. Lucky for me she walks over to her car alone.

"Hey miss? Do you know where I could find a decent hotel for the night?" I ask her.

She looks me up and down and I see the flirty little smile curve her luscious lips. "There is one, two blocks away on the left hand side." She seems like she is going to be easy.

I look her up and down in an obvious way that shows I want a piece of her "Would you be interested in showing me the way?" I say in invitation.

Her smile grows wider. "I suppose I can do that."

On the way over we talk about her of course as I am trying to lure her up to my bedroom where I can debauch her. She prattles on about her dance class and I smile in all the right places, not listening to a damn thing she says. After using a little demonic persuasion I get her up to my room where I continue to rock her world. She really was a beautiful little thing and I felt bad about proceeding to devour her soul leaving her cold and lifeless. Her innocence strengthens me and her lack of malice has more power than it is given credit for. It's too bad I had to kill her for it. Wait, did I feel guilt for doing something I have done for thousands of years? I hope Angus isn't rubbing off on me.

When I get back home, I see that Sirens lights are on and I decide to go invisible and check on the woman unlike any other. She is lying on her couch asleep and looking more gorgeous than anyone has the right to. I go over to her and brush my fingers along her cheek. I don't know why I feel so drawn to her, but it must be her unnatural power, or maybe it's her soul. Maybe it's because she is the first woman to ever have turned me down.

Her face suddenly scrunches up like she is in pain and she starts muttering incoherently. All of a sudden I hear, "You can't... No..." and then she sighs and her face relaxes. I don't know what happened to this woman, but there is most certainly more to her than meets the eye.

I feel a pang... of something as I watch her and remember the guilt I felt earlier after devouring that young woman's soul for my own selfish need for more strength, more power... always more. I haven't felt guilt, or any real emotion since I was a young demon. I wasn't always like this, killing for sport simply because I can. I used to loath who I was because I was always told that killing was part of my nature which I had to embrace rather than reject. I never really could though.

My lack of desire to kill, torture and maim were considered a weakness in my father's eyes. Every time he looked at me, all I could see was the disappointment that I couldn't be crueler, more like him.

One evening he took me out to the biggest village he could find and told me to kill a young couple. I cried, I didn't want to do it. I didn't even want to think about spilling the blood of those who were so obviously in love. He laughed at my weakness and dragged me into the house where the couple lived. He slaughtered them in the most gruesome of ways and then he turned on me and beat me until I was broken and bloodied. He left me to suffer, but not die in a pool of my own blood and that of his two other victims.

This soon turned into a game that he clearly enjoyed. I either killed a couple or he killed them anyway, then beat me to the brink of death as well. I don't even know how long this lasted, or how many victims were never given mercy because of my unwillingness to kill them myself.

One day I finally did it, knowing that whether I pulled the trigger or not they were going to die and maybe by my hand it would be less painful. I thought of it as a kindness that my father would not bestow on them. So I made myself kill an entire family, and I hated myself for it. Like many of the mortals I have met over the years have said, the first time is the hardest. Unfortunately, after that it got easier and easier until one day, I could do it without feeling at all.

I hear a soft sigh and look at the beauty before me as she lies there unaware of the danger in her house with her. I wonder what it is that has made her into the woman she has become and if her story is as tragic as mine. It's hard to think of anyone hurting this gorgeous creature who looks so small and fragile, yet owns so much power.

As I watch her sleep I remember the angels who told me I was never good enough and assumed that because of my bloodline that I was innately evil. Maybe they were right, maybe not, but thanks to my father we will never know if I could have been something different, someone different. Since I have known Siren, I have felt a few emotions, maybe it's because of her tear the other day. Maybe it's because of something else. Maybe both.

All I really know for sure is that I want her with a ferocity I have never felt before. I think about her continuously and it's driving me crazy. I don't know what she did to Angus or if he is just much weaker than I thought, but I know that she could very possibly bring a man to his knees.

After watching her for a little longer I get up and go back to my own place where I am away from the temptation that is Siren.

(EZEKIEL)

I don't know what to think of Siren. One second she is a demon and the next a complete angel. It's enough to hurt my head. Eating and talking to her, getting to know her, there truly is something enthralling about her. I can see why Daemon has so much interest in the little siren. A laugh comes out of my mouth with the thought that her name is appropriate for the creature herself. I would say that could be what she is if there were such a thing, plus I never heard her sing.

I couldn't keep my eyes off of her for long because the sad fact is that she is easy on the eyes. The thought of any kind of attraction disgusts me, I cannot be attracted to a woman I myself may have to kill. She clearly has no problem with ending lives, but then she can put a smile on a young girls face in less than an hour apart. I don't understand it.

At least I know that I will be able to get another date out of her and smile at the prospect. I will get to know her better. Maybe I can get under her skin enough for her to let her guard down just enough for me to see what she really is underneath the beauty and the power. Maybe than I can determine if the magnificent creature will need to be put down.

If not, maybe I can get her to join my army. I feel a smug smile at having this vixen on my team where I can admire her up close and personal. I shake my head not knowing where such a thought has come from. I don't want to admire the vile woman, but then I remember her smile and I think it might not be such a burden. Dammit, I need to stop this right now. If I have to kill her it won't really matter how lovely she seems. There will be nothing in the world that will stop me.

I go over the events of the night, talking and laughing with her. Being around her was too easy and that makes me feel uncomfortable now. A woman who can kill a man and walk away like nothing happened, shouldn't be so easy to be around. I have to find out what she is hiding, where she is from, why she came here and why she sounded like it wasn't by choice. Who is this enigmatic woman?

For many millennia I have saved innocents, eliminate evil and not once seen anything like her. I have followed Daemon and tried to intervene whenever possible, never being able to eradicate him from this world. Neither of us can ever quite outwit the other one no matter how hard either of us try. Regardless of anything when it comes to Siren, maybe I can use her to my advantage before any final decision is made.

EVERY NOW AND THEN I like to sit at the highest vantage point and watch everything happen below. I try to save the souls that I can, but there are times when it truly isn't worth the effort. There comes a time when we have to cut our losses. That's also my number one reason I seldom go to that demon filled club to save anyone. Yes, there are plenty of people who go there for a night of fun who would never dabble into anything dark. Unfortunately, the vast majority are tainted. It's late now, and it's a weekday so there aren't as many people wandering around.

Something catches my eye, so I turn invisible and fly down to check it out. A middle aged woman is milling around and something about this situation feels very wrong. A man walks out of the building she's standing in front of, but turns to walk in the direction away from her, and she follows him. I follow her. As we walk, I can feel the hostility wafting off of her in waves and I know she is going to do something awful.

"You thought you could sneak around on me did you?" She yells to the man, and he turns around slowly with a mix of surprise and fear on his face.

"I... uh... don't know what you're talking about." he stammers out.

"Oh yeah? Pretty red head, about yay high." She holds her hand just below her own eye level making this other woman about five foot nothing. "And I am pretty sure the last time I saw her she was wrapped around you like boa." He slowly backs away from her, also sensing her malice. She then pulls out a gun and points it toward the man and he throws up his hands in surrender.

"Judy, we broke up two months ago because you were always jealous of other woman." He swallows hard.

She laughs a little maniacally. "You cannot leave me you bastard!" She shrieks the last word. I can tell she is going to pull the trigger so I intervene. She pulls the trigger and as the bullet is whizzing towards its target, a blast of light comes from the palm of my hand, blinding the couple and disintegrating the bullet. She is looking around, not knowing what just happened as he's looking at himself, checking for holes.

I finally appear between the two of them, standing sideways with my hands out toward each of them. Looking at him I say "You go home." with that he turns and runs off. I turn to face her and say, "You are coming with me." I grab her by the arm and fly her to the local police department. She isn't tainted by a demon, therefore there is nothing as an angel I can do about it, but I can make sure that the human authorities take care of her.

On my way back to the little apartment I decided to rent, I get a 'call' that I have to go to the club after all.

I get there and there is fire being thrown around at one another. Some of them are obviously demonic and others look like fire crackers or some such crap.

I look around at the carnage and see a group of people in their early twenties hovering over in a corner. They look terrified and are definitely not a part of this group. I march over to them while dodging fire, ducking and side stepping when needed.

"Let's get you guys out of here." I say to the small group. There are three girls and two guys. I see a fire exit not too far away from me and I get the group to get behind me as much as possible as we slowly slip out. I get them out the door, when I see that there are more people who aren't a part of this battle.

Before I can do anything about it, Daemon busts through the doors and the look in his eyes is lethal. "What the fuck is going on?" and as he says it, an inferno comes from his hands and vanquishes a large group of demons. "Anyone who comes here to cause mass chaos like this again is going to end up like those guys. Everyone understand? I don't care if you are a fucking human." He glares at everyone in the room. "Everyone out." and people start to slowly disperse out the doors. "Now!" he roars.

I have never seen him express such rage, or really any real emotion. Even when he kills it's with a nonchalance that is greatly unnerving. I have seen other demons kill with glee, giddy over the evil they have created, but not Daemon. Over the thousands of years I have seen the wars he has created, souls he has sucked, women he has bedded and never has he shown even the slightest hint of emotion over any of it. Sure when he seduces a woman he puts forth the effort to be perceived as someone who gives a shit, but really he just wants to get laid. His little demon calls a lot of the shots and is probably the only part of him that feels anything at all.

I turn away from him and sneak out the back, I don't want him alerted that I'm here quite yet.

(DAEMON)

I look around my club, seething as I look at the destruction those fucktards have made. I had one rule and that was not to cause a scene and there was definitely a scene created. Now I have a mess to clean up, some demons to replace and never mind the humans who were not a part of the clubs theme. I might have to hunt them down and kill them. I would really rather not because that would create a bigger scene.

If a bunch of young adults go missing or their bodies are found, that is going to alert the cops and I really don't want to have to deal with that headache.

I rub my hands down my face, "What am I going to do?" I grumble. Siren seems to have powers of unidentified origins, but I doubt she would help me. She really doesn't seem to like me much. On the other hand it would give me the opportunity to talk to her, I think smiling with evil intent. Okay, but I can't exactly tell her why I need her help and I don't really want to reveal that I know she is different from the humans here. Huh, how am I going to get her to help me?

(Siren)

I wake up from a sleep that was not disturbed by my chronically horny next door neighbour. I feel well rested and ready for my day. Thank God today is Saturday. Maybe I will go by the river I love so much and restore my magic to its fullest. This week has been overly draining, what with the killing and the maiming. Oh and I can't forget about the emasculation of that one man who showed up at Daemons the other night.

I get to the river and take off my clothes and decide I am going to swim in the nude. No one comes here and it is something I quite enjoy doing. I close my eyes and center myself on all the life around me and exchange energy with the plants. I look around and again the plants are more vibrant as per usual. I dive into the water and swim out a little before I come back up. The quiet of the place is peaceful even though its quietness still contains the music of the birds and insects. Within the silence I hear a snap of a twig and I hold my breath while looking around.

"Well, well, swimming in the buff." I sigh loudly as I look at the offending voice, offensive by nature I'm sure.

"Did you follow me here?" I ask completely exasperated.

Daemon shrugs with a sly smile. "I just happened to go for a walk in the same direction as you."

"Well if you don't mind you can find your way back." Unfortunately he starts peeling of his clothes and throwing them on the ground. He takes off his underwear and I spin around as quickly as possible, but not before seeing him in all his glory. Dammit, why does he have to be so fine? And so irritating?

"Oh Si, don't be like that" he says mockingly.

"Do not call me Si, my name is Siren you stupid arrogant..." and my words are cut off by the sounds of him getting in the water and swimming towards me. I turn back to face him. "I am not going to have that peaceful morning I was so hoping for am I?"

"You can still have that, just pretend I'm not even here." He swims under the water away from me. Grr, should I leave? No I can't let him win, he's antagonising me. Challenging me. He wants to get a rise from me and I'll be damned before that happens.

I watch him as he swims and damn I have to admit (begrudgingly) that he has a nice body. A six pack, some nice muscles, without looking like a weight lifter on steroids. He turns around and I know I have been caught red handed. I just roll my eyes and turn away to continue on with my swimming.

"So Siren, I hear you have a penchant for ripping out hearts." he says out of the blue.

I slowly turn toward him. "Is that the rumour on the street these days? I can assure you, I am sure I have broken many hearts, I have yet to actually rip one out." I say on a laugh. "Is that what your idiot friend accused me of?"

"Yes, but there were many other people who beat him to the punch."

"Yes, drunks are usually the most reliable sources of information. I'm sure they see a lot of things at that disgusting club of yours." I throw at him.

"Okay, I'll accept that, but what about the man in the alley way? The one whose face you burned with your blood?" He throws back at me casually as if he were talking about what he ate for supper... maybe even more casually than that. I stiffen at that because he laughs darkly. "That's right, you didn't think anyone saw that little stunt now did you?"

I turn back to him. "What do you want Daemon?" I say with bite.

"I have a problem. A few people saw something they shouldn't have at my club last night, I was hoping that maybe you could use you're magical mojo and make them forget, lest I have to kill them.

"What did they see?" I respond sharply to him. How dare he try to get leverage on me. The bastard.

"That is none of your concern. You are going to help me because if you don't, I will make sure everyone knows you're a little... less than human." In a demanding tone that says 'I will get what I want no matter what I have to do to get it'.

"Since you put it so eloquently, I think I am going to have to decline your offer." I retort flippantly and I hear a growl from behind me. "Is that all? Because I would really like to continue my swim in peace." I look over at him and he has a stance that says 'I'm not going anywhere'. "Alone" I add in way to tell him to get lost.

"You know this is a great swimming hole. I think I might stay a while." He then dives under the water. Dammit, what will it take for him to leave? As he comes back up he grins, "I wonder how many other people would love to come swimming here since I'm sure it isn't common knowledge." He sounds as if he is deeply contemplating the question. "You wouldn't be able swim in the nude, though I do appreciate the look." He's clearly looking at my breast as he licks his lips suggestively.

"Then I will make my past punishments look like a sugar coated treat in comparison to what I will do to you." I say as lightly as I can muster. "Do not threaten me, I am not afraid of being... exposed... besides, other than the lake, no one will believe you." The best part about this world is no one believes anything they can't personally understand or comprehend.

"As I said, I have witnesses." he shoots back angrily. "If you don't help me out here, not only will I ruin your carefully perceived reputation but I will make your life a living hell... literally. I do have the power to do it. You aren't the only one less than human." His face darkens and the smile says he isn't lying about it. "I will kill an innocent witness from last night every day that you make me wait for an answer. This was to save face after all. I don't care much about their puny human lives." He gets out of the water and puts on his clothes. "I guess I have to go and track one of them down now." With that he walks away, but not before throwing, "Maybe she'll be a good lay." over his shoulder.

I hate him. I mean I have never wanted to punch a hole through someone's chest more badly than I do his at this very moment. The thought of his ending of innocent life sends a spark of panic through me. He wouldn't kill anyone just to teach me a lesson would he? Surely he even has one scruple right? I suddenly realize I don't really know him but I have a bad feeling churning in my gut.

I GET HOME AND I'M not there fifteen minutes before I hear the very familiar sound from next door. I march over to his apartment muttering, "I'm going to flay him like a fish. No maybe I'll gut him like one... or maybe I'll rip out his heart like I did his friend." I knock on the door and as I do the sound stops right after a thump sounds against a wall.

I open the door which was surprisingly unlocked to find him standing over a now unconscious but dressed woman in a skirt and him doing up his pants. That explains the last thump.

"Well it's nice of you to finally join me. This is Sarah. She was at my club the other night. She isn't quite an innocent, I can see that now, but I don't think that she should die for being so easy." He grins at me and it's full of wicked intent. "I would like to have a round two with her since we didn't get to finish before you arrived, but you know... priorities." He looks back at the girl. "Sadly though, that won't save her life... but you can".

Dammit, he would kill a witness. "Fine." I say on a frustrated sigh. "I'll help you, but if I ever need your help then you better deliver."

I march over to the girl and check her pulse and it's still strong. Good. I stretch out my arm with my hand strangling him with my magic and insuring he can't move to fight me. "But if so much as one of these people are hurt or killed, whether directly from you or not, I will kill you in the most painful of ways. Do. You. Understand?" For once I see a bit of fear in his eyes, but he nods and I release him. I touch the girls head and erase all signs of Daemon from her mind.

"She won't remember you at all so she won't recall this... dalliance. Give me a list of people you want me to mind fuck and I'll get on it." With that I walk back to my place, close the door and hope I don't get involved in anymore of his lunacy.

(Daemon)

Shit, that did not go as planned at all. I didn't want her to know that I suspected her powers, and I definitely didn't want to be on the receiving end of them. That was frightening and I do not scare easily. I rub my throat for I can still feel the burn there.

I look down at Sarah on the floor and realize I am going to have to move her or explain how she got into my house with no recollection as to how. Dammit, I really wanted another round with this one. I guess I'll have to seduce her again later. I pick her up and in a blink she is back to her house where I so gallantly seduced her back to my house. I set her on her couch, and leave her there still unconscious from me bashing her head on the wall when I heard Siren at my door.

The thought of *her* drives me with a deep seeded lust that makes me want to possess and devour. She is the one I truly crave and all the other woman are a cheap imitation. She is a challenge I desperately need to win, God so desperately. It was so *hard* to control myself when I was with her at the lake. All that naked beauty out there for just anyone to leer at. And leer I did as I watched her from a bush before I divulged my presence. Oh how I wanted to back her into the water and wrap her sexy little body around mine. I moan at the thought. Okay this is getting seriously out of hand. I look down at 'Little Daemon' and say "Don't worry, we'll quench your desire for her, through fair means or foul".

I look back at Sarah lying peacefully on the couch and I know I should leave, but for some reason I can't just walk away. I check her head to make sure it isn't too badly damaged and for some reason I feel a sense of... something... relief? Tenderness? It has been many millennia since I have felt anything other than lust, violence and the lust for violence.

This isn't right and I stand up abruptly, trying to push the younger woman out of my mind who can't be any older than twenty five. She isn't going to die and Siren is going to help me. That is all that matters. I know why the latter one matters which is because I don't want any suspicion to land on me, but as for the former? I haven't got the strangest idea.

I go back to my place and write up the list of the people who were at the club. Most of the witnesses were in their early twenties. Most of them were women, but there were still quite a few men. After writing the list, I go over to Siren's and knock on her door. Thankfully she answers, but she looks none too happy to see me. "I have that list for you." I explain before she can slam the door in my face.

"That was fast." She holds out her hand in way of demand. I give it to her and she looks it over. "Okay, there are twenty seven names on here, it will take me a few days but I will erase their memory of you."

"Good. Tell me when you are done." I walk back to my place. Every damn time I see her I want to push her up against something. This time she was wearing sweat pants and a T-shirt and I still wanted to ravage her. I take a deep breath. I decide that I'm going to go invisible and watch her.

I go over and watch her lounging on her couch, looking over the names on her list and then setting the list aside and turning on the television. I lean on the back of the couch and catch a whiff of her hair. How I want to bury my face in that and inhale her in. Her skin looks soft and lick-able. What is wrong with me, I am definitely having some sort of internal dilemma here.

Usually I just think about sating my desire and that's that. I have to get out of here before she somehow gets under my skin enough to convince me that my lifestyle is dangerous and immoral. I shiver at the idea and go back to my apartment. Siren is the biggest threat to me.

(Ezekiel)

Siren is doing the demon's bidding. How naïve. I watch her as she goes and visits every person on that list and erases Daemon from their memories. She does it so easily, so effortlessly. I don't know what caused her to do it. Maybe she slept with him and he talked her into it. Sounds like the Daemon thing to do. Every being between heaven and hell knows what Daemon is like. Some of them seek him for their pleasure. Did Siren? I shake away the thought.

She finishes the list and goes back to Daemon's place and she hands him the list of her duties. The look he gives her as she walks away can only be described as scorching. "Hey Siren." Even I can hear the seduction in his tone. "Would you like to come inside? We could discuss how it went saving all those people."

Saving. As if he would even understand the definition. I am pretty sure he considers saving a life as not killing them. In fact I bet I am right on the money with this one. "Um, well, everyone is alive and none of them remember you, there is no need to come inside."

He chuckles. "Afraid you won't be able to control yourself if you're left alone with me?"

"Actually that is exactly what I'm afraid of." I feel a dark emotion at that. "I am afraid I won't be able to control this deep desire I have." She is sleeping with him. "To not only beat you to a pulp, but to then watch as you slowly bleed out." I look up at her a little shocked by her words. A little too happy that she isn't sleeping with Daemon even though I might still have to kill her. At least it doesn't have to be right now. It gives me time to wine and dine her and figure out what on earth she is. Maybe I will have to stop by her house unexpectedly.

I KNOCK ON HER DOOR with flowers that I picked myself, thinking she might appreciate that, women can be so sentimental. She opens the door with a look of irritation, but pauses when she sees me. A smile slowly spreads across her lovely face. "I was wondering if you wanted to go out for supper with me tonight." I watch as she contemplates and chews her lip in thought.

"I don't know, I had a busy day today..."

"We will have a nice dinner and you can relax with good company. How does that sound?"

She smiles a little. "I suppose I can do that, but I can't be out too late or I'll turn into a pumpkin".

He grins. "Fair enough." I hold out my hand to her.

"While we are talking about spells, I think I need one done on my rags." She pulls her hand away. "Do you mind waiting a few minutes for me to change into something a little more decent?"

Not long after she comes out, but decent is not the word I would use to describe the outfit she is wearing. It is a deep crimson halter top and blue jean short shorts. I gulp and try to push back indecent thoughts. I can't help but look her up and down and damn, if she doesn't drip with sex appeal. No wonder Daemon was looking at her like that. I am happy he isn't here to see her now. I can't forget the plan, to figure her out and possibly destroy her.

We get to the restaurant, and as we walk through, I see she is the centre of attention. We finally make it to our seat. "Wow, looks like the women love you." She says with amusement.

"Well than you're lucky that I already made my choice for a date this evening." To which she laughs, the sound so light and carefree.

"Well then, I should do them a service and decline next time because I'm such a Good Samaritan like that." She has a crooked smile but her words remind me how far from the truth that is.

"Do you like to do any good deeds?" I ask soberly.

"Yes. I love my volunteer work. I get to know that a couple times a week, that I can truly make a difference in someone else's life." For a moment I see her eyes light up like nothing I have ever seen before.

"There are a lot of ways to change someone's life." I spit out darkly and a strange look crosses her face, but it happens so fast that I'm not sure what I saw. It wasn't guilt that's for sure, but there was something there. She turns her eyes to the table cloth and then she looks back up at me.

"Sometimes doing things for the greater good are harder than others." She shrugs it off. The waitress comes and we order a champagne along with our meals.

The rest of the meal goes by and we talk and laugh. I hate to admit it, but being with her is easy and quite enjoyable. Hopefully my duty won't be problematic.

After we eat I take her to another part of the restaurant where there is a dance floor and a bar and people are already dancing and having a great time. No one is dancing provocatively as this is a high class place, but you can tell they didn't need to in order to have a good time. We were dancing for an hour when Siren says she needs a break.

She goes over to the bar and orders us a drink. I don't indulge much so I figured 'what the hell' so to speak.

On her way back, a young woman elbows her out of her way. All I can think is this is the end. Our night is going to be ruined, which was surprisingly enjoyable. Shall I even dare say fun?

I see Siren's mischievous grin and know she is going to make a blow. She slightly holds out her leg and the woman trips, catching herself with her other foot, but still spilling the contents of her drink. She turns toward Siren. "You Bitch."

Siren's smile widens as she says "And you best remember that." She continues on her way in my direction. I was shocked that it didn't end in too much violence, especially death.

As we are dancing on the floor, I notice that people seem drawn to her dancing. Maybe her name Siren isn't too far off the mark. I wonder if she can sing. Even though she isn't dancing too provocative, there seems to be a natural allure about her. She's like an enigma that I just can't seem to figure out. She is cruel, yet kind. Sweet, funny, sarcastic and blunt. I can't figure her out and it's more than a little unnerving.

"What was that about?" I point my head in the other woman's direction.

"Women! They are always the same, everywhere you go." When she looks up at me she shakes her a head a little. "More than a little cray-cray." With a look behind her at the other woman, "Some more than others".

"Yes..." I say slowly. "But that doesn't answer the question"

"She's a crazy woman. Who knows what that was about. It could have been from anything to not liking the look of me, to really liking the look of you. Hell it could have been the fact she thought I was prettier than her. Or she liked my shoes... seriously... you can never be too sure." She ends on a huff.

"So basically, no matter my confidence in my ability to understand a woman, I will never really do so?"

To that she laughs. "Confidence in that will just give her more power to undermine you."

"Oh yeah? How so?"

"It's not really a lesson that can be taught through explanation so much as through experience."

"What about you?" Maybe I can have some insight into this particular woman.

"Me? I'm more calculating than most. It's not so much that I want to deceive, so much as I think through my actions to achieve the more favourable result."

"Favourable to whom?"

"Whomever the situation warrants." She takes my hand. "Now let's go dance." She drags me to the floor again and wraps her arms around my neck. I can feel her body against mine as she dances to a song that has a fast pace. I can feel her hips dancing to the beat. I try to dance as well but I am distracted by her. Not just the fact that she is so close to me, but just by her as a being. She is so complex that it leaves me disoriented.

(DAEMON)

Siren seems to have cleaned up my problem quickly and much more efficiently than I would have thought possible. I was hoping it would give me a chance to get to know her better. Seeing her at the water in the nude, it took everything in me not to try to seduce her, but I know it wouldn't have worked, not on this woman.

I go to my club to... I don't want to say baby-sit, but that is essentially what I am here to do. I want to make sure that what happened the other night does not happen again.

There are so many beautiful women here tonight, so many to sate my need and yet after spending more time with Siren, I realize that none of them can really compare. Maybe it's the challenge she presents, or maybe it's because I want her like I have no other, either way it's my goal to win her. I see a prior conquest walking my way and I know what she wants after how I made her scream last time, and yet the thought does nothing for me.

"Hey sexy." She leers as she walks up to me. She runs one finger from the base of my neck down my chest and then lower, until she gets much, much lower. "Want to go back to one of the back rooms you have? Maybe this time I can please you." I grab her hands from my pant button before she can do anything further.

"You pleased me plenty last time, but I am here for business, not pleasure." I tell her in my most dominant voice that warrants no further argument.

"But I'm not wearing any underwear." she purrs.

Admittedly, that is a hard image to eradicate from my mind, but I still say, "I have to make sure everyone here behaves themselves. Now go play with one of the other men here tonight because you won't be playing with me." She stomps away like I took away her favourite toy. Maybe I did.

I walk around the club, watching the gyrating of hips as men and women dance like they are in a private bedroom. I watch as the corrupted who come here try to get the innocents to follow their lead, making my job a lot easier in the process. For some reason, the seeing of this doesn't give me the satisfaction that it should have, the kind I would normally feel.

I see women offering younger women cocaine, trying to loosen them up. Men doing the same thing for the same purpose, but for an entirely different reason. My club is a place with a lack of inhibition. It's a place that any demon should be proud of, as I have witnessed many times all the people who come here for one sole reason, and that is to lose themselves. Whether it be, booze, drugs, sex or something else, they come here to do it.

I wonder if I could get Siren to loosen up and lose herself a little if I brought her here. I know she has been here before, but she wasn't here with me. If I could seduce her than maybe I could be done with this constant craving I have for her. I'm not sure what she is doing to me, but I think about her far too often. When I get the opportunity to see her or rile her up, I can't help but take it. Maybe I should take home a woman and make sure we are as loud as possible just so she will come by and tell me off. I smile at the cunning of it but there is no one here who catches my fancy, which is extremely unusual.

I look around the crowd and I see so many souls that I have corrupted for my army, even though they have no idea what kind of fall they have really taken. They don't know that the only purpose I really have for them is to eventually die in a fight that may never be won.

I continue my perusal of the club when I see a bright soul, one that could feed me and make me stronger. I watch as she declines most of the attention around her and I study her. Maybe she could help me with my frustrations before I kill her. She walks over to her friends and she says something with so much animation that I can't help but laugh a little. Suddenly I feel a pang that I have never felt before. Guilt? Distress? Definitely distress because whatever the feeling is, I find it incredibly distressing. I turn away from the girl and continue my journey around the club.

I walk by a couple of demons arguing but they stop as soon as they spot me and look sheepishly away. I guess word travels fast about how I feel about misconduct in here. They disperse immediately after I pass. Good, they should be afraid.

I GO HOME, IT'S THE first time in forever that I can remember, that I went home without taking a woman. I'm not sure what that says about me because I have a pretty insatiable appetite. I go to bed and fall asleep quickly.

I can't remember the last time I fell right to sleep or the last time I dreamt, but tonight I did both.

I was looking around at all the other demon children who were so excited to go out for their first hunt. To kill and manipulate, to learn from their fathers. Me, I wasn't interested at all, I just wanted to stay home.

"Listen, you must go, you have to have this rite of passage as we have all done"

"I don't want to kill people, I don't want to be a demon"

"Now son, you are going to go out into the field and you are going to do as you are told. No more arguments or it will be you who will be killed"

I went with him but I never killed, I couldn't do it. I had plenty of opportunities, but I did my best to play it off as just being "to slow" or "not stealthy enough". Eventually I was taken back home and my dad was furious. He beat me and tortured me until I was all too close to losing consciousness, and then he said, "If you don't start becoming what you were meant to be, the next beating will be far worse".

Next I saw faces, hundreds of faces, maybe thousands... maybe more. Some, I could see clearly, some not so much. Some I could hear their screams of agony, their cries for help and their pleas for mercy. But none of it would save them.

I startle awake in a cold sweat and look around the room for an attacker or for whatever had awaken me in that state. Then I remember the dream. I lie back down thinking about it. I haven't thought about that day in more millennia's than I could even count. The day my father started molding me into what I am today. That memory was so much more than just a memory though, it was a reminder that I didn't always want to be this. I wonder what that small boy would think of me now.

Chapter Five

(Siren)

I am working at the flower shop, putting together some orders for an upcoming wedding, even though I don't have the whole order as of yet. I am putting together the little that I have. The arrangement is gorgeous if I must say so myself... and I must, plus I love the colours that this particular bride picked. I have always been a fan of the 'in your face' vibrant colours. I love that she chose to have a mixture of scarlet, fuchsia, magenta, azure, rose and apricot. I think the bride might even have said something about her dress following some eccentric colour scheme.

I am focussing on making the best arrangements I can when I hear the bell ring above my door. I go out to find a beautiful young woman standing there and she is looking at the flowers I have around my shop. Finally she turns to look at me and her smile is so bright I can't help but smile back.

"I was just wondering if you would be able to make fifteen arrangements for me. I want them to be bright and happy. I definitely want some sun flowers in there along with some purple irises and blue daisies."

"I am pretty sure that can be arranged, how soon do you need them?"

"By tonight if that's possible. That is possible right? I know, I know I shouldn't have waited until the last second, but I do tend to procrastinate."

"That's fine" I say with a smile to ease her. "I happen to have those flowers on hand."

She sighs with relief "Thank you. How much will that be?" She pays the bill and says she will be back by five to pick up the order. I am going to be busy with this, but it gives me something to do at least. Hopefully that will stop me from thinking about the date I had last night and how it was surprisingly a lot of fun.

As I am getting the arrangements together, I sense a dark presence around me. I look around, but I don't see anyone. I continue on my way but that feeling that something isn't right nags in the back of my mind.

LATER ON I DECIDE THAT tonight I will go to the homeless shelter and help out since I didn't have any plans tonight anyway. I walk into the place and I see a familiar flower arrangements on all of the tables, all fifteen of them. Damn, I wasn't expecting that.

I walk into the kitchen and there is a new face, but one I recognize from earlier that day.

"Hey, so this is why you needed those arrangements pronto huh?" I ask her.

She twirls around on me with a knife in her hand and it looks like she was cutting up vegetables for dinner. "Yeah, I thought this place needed a little pick me up." She turns back to what she was doing.

"I'm Siren by the way." I walk over to her and pick up another knife and start helping her with cutting some other vegetables that happen to be waiting in turn.

She looks over at me and smiles that bright smile again. "I'm Annabelle, but you can call be Anna if you like." She continues with the chopping. While we are working together, I get to know this girl a lot better. She is new in town and loves helping the community when she can.

I get that dark feeling again and I look around, but again there is no one I can see around me. It's incredibly unnerving, but I continue my shift volunteering as I did at work all day long. Trying to ignore the feeling in my gut that says something isn't right.

I GET HOME, BUT DURING the entire walk there I felt something that I couldn't shake no matter what. I finally sit down in my living room when I hear a knock on the door. I answer it and Zeek is there so I let him in.

"I know I probably should have called but I thought maybe I could interest you with some dinner?" He holds up some Chinese takeout. "And a bottle of wine?"

"Free food and alcohol? Who would say no to that?" I reply with a smile and let him in. "To what do I owe the pleasure?"

"I had a good time last night and thought I would come by and continue it tonight." He smiles at me in a way that makes me tingle.

"Okay, set that down on the table and I will get some glasses for the wine." He does as I say and starts unpacking them from the bag. We eat, talk and laugh, and I realize I'm happy that he came by tonight. It's nice to be distracted from that feeling that has been following me all day.

The distraction doesn't last long as I look around after feeling a chill seeping through my bones. I notice Zeek is looking around as well, but doing so more subtly than I. I give him a smile I don't feel and continue to eat. The mood isn't ruined for long as he starts asking me about my day. I tell him about the girl who bought flowers from me to bring to the shelter that I like to volunteer at.

"It's nice to know there is still some good in this world." He looks at me as if he's scrutinising me as he says it.

"Yeah it really is. Sometimes I start to doubt it." I look away from his gaze.

"Surely that isn't true if you can help the hungry alongside others." When I look up I see he is looking at his plate as he stabs chicken and shoves it in his mouth.

"Yes, it does restore faith, until I look around and see all the people who can't be bothered." This time when I look up, he is looking at me with interest and maybe a little confusion as well.

"Well. where there is good there is always going to be indifference and evil." He cocks his head as he looks at me.

"Well evil is a whole other thing all together. When I look around this town I see so much of it. It wasn't always like this you know. When I first moved here it was a lot quieter." I take a sip of my wine in thought. "It seems that it has become infested with snakes recently when I come to think of it." I set my wine down and shake the thought away.

We eat the rest of our dinner and have a few glasses of wine while talking some more. As it gets later I decide that we should watch a movie or something I mean what woman wouldn't want to be in the presence of some serious eye candy anyway? I am in no rush for him to leave. As I sit down in the living room, something catches my eye on the coffee table. A note in an envelope with my name on it.

Curiously I open it up and freeze as my breath gets caught in my throat.

Siren,

You looked beautiful today in your disguise, but it will take more than that to lose me. Just remember how well I know you. I do hope you enjoyed the Chinese food with your *friend*.

Love always.

I look at the letter and even though he didn't sign his name, I know exactly who it is from.

"Siren are you alright?" He goes to take the letter from me.

I pull it back from him, crumple it up and throw it in the trash. "It's nothing." I say. I turn on a movie but I don't really watch any of it as my heart races. I'm in danger.

(DAEMON)

I came home today to the sound of laughter next door. I must say Siren has a gorgeous laugh. She has a gorgeous everything. Some more laughter and then some murmuring and I recognize one voice to be male. I swear my heart stopped in my chest at the sound. She sounds like she's having a good time, unfortunately not long after, everything goes very, very quiet.

My fists are clenched as I try not to think about what is or isn't going on next door. There had better not be anything going on over there. I go downstairs to a gym I put in my basement. Luckily I also have a punching bag and I beat the shit out of the thing. I fight until my knuckles are bloody before I go back upstairs.

I hear some more talking next door and I try to eavesdrop. I hear her say good night and that she will walk him to the car. Finally I get to see the sonofabitch I'm going to murder.

I watch her as she walks outside with him and right when they arrive at his car, he turns to her and smiles down, resting his hand on her face. I can't see him very well even though he is facing my direction because of the shadows across his face. He leans down and kisses her and there is something boiling inside of me. Then she puts her arm around his neck and kisses him back. An anger like no other burns through me and I want to march out there and kill the bastard.

Finally they come up for air and I can finally see his face. Ezekiel. He looks up at me and winks before turning to go to his car. What the hell does he want with Siren?

I grab my keys and jump in my car speeding off and go to my club. I'll be able to unwind there or at the very least, drink 'til I don't care. I go to the bar and immediately order a few shots.

"You okay boss?" the bartender asks me and I just shoot her a dark glare in answer. After the shots I go and dance with some women, but even that doesn't make me feel any better. Just when I thought I couldn't feel worse, I hear "about time you showed up." and I freeze at the sound of the familiar voice. One voice I haven't heard in a couple hundred years. I slowly turn around and there she is. Gwendolyn.

"What the hell are you doing here?" I snap at her.

"I missed you." she purrs and I remember her seductions as she circles my lips with her finger. I slap her hand away and I glare down at her.

"What are you doing here? I am only going to ask one more time." and her smile fades.

"Like I said, I missed you and wanted to see you okay? Is that really so bad?"

"Yes! You made your feelings very clear when you left."

"That was two hundred years ago, feelings fade."

"Not yours." I growl at her.

She rolls her eyes at me. "A woman's prerogative is known for changing." She takes my hand and walks me to the dance floor where she starts to grind against me. I lightly push her away from me and walk back to the bar. How could tonight have gone so horribly wrong?

"I remember a time when you would have taken that as an invitation."

"That was a very long time ago" I retort.

"What is wrong with you?" she snaps at me and then I see a dawning in her eyes. "It's a woman isn't it?" and her eyes darken. "You found a woman? Have you forgotten the prophesy?"

"No I have not, I just decided that if I'm going to be destroyed, I might as well enjoy the time I have left. That does not include you." I walk out of the bar. I need to get away somewhere. First, Ezekiel kissing Siren and her more than enjoying it and now Gwendolyn. I am going to need a hell of a lot more than a stiff drink and a good lay.

I COULD PROBABLY THINK of a million things that would make me feel better, but right now I don't feel like doing any of them. I go back to my house and I see Siren's lights are on.

I go inside and I see light illuminating the back yard, and I recall how much she likes being out there. I slide open my door and walk outside, and for the first time, the look I see on her face is not one of happiness or snark. She looks desolate in a way that I didn't even know she could feel. When she looks up at me she smiles but it's so forced and fake it pains me.

"Are you alright?" I ask quietly.

She doesn't answer right away, just looks back down at the ground and takes a deep breath "Honestly? I have no idea." I notice her hands are shaking but she tries to hide it. "I got a letter tonight and I think I might be in trouble"

I laugh at that. "I have seen how strong you are. It would take someone pretty powerful to take you down." That's when she looks at me and I see it in her face. "Oh shit, they're stronger than you are aren't they?" and she just nods her head at me.

"Anything I can do?" I ask her, with high hopes that there is something that I can do, but she just shakes her head and looks back at the ground.

"There isn't anything anyone can do." With that she gets up and walks to her sliding glass door. "Thanks for the company but I think I'm just going to go inside and sulk." Then she is gone.

I don't know what happened between seeing her with the angel and now, but I wish more than anything I could take it away. I know that feeling goes against everything that makes me a demon but it is what it is.

I WAKE UP FROM A RESTLESS sleep because I can't get Siren's look of sadness out of my mind or the kiss with that damned angel. Okay not damned... yet. I decide I am going to try to redeem her perception of me so I am going to make breakfast for her. I look in the fridge and realize it's empty. It would have been a lot easier if I didn't have to go to the store and buy supplies, but for some reason I feel like I have to. What is wrong with me?

I go to the store and pick up some eggs, bacon and some crescents that are premade. I take them up to the cashier and pay for them. Before I know it I'm back home cooking breakfast. I don't cook often but when I do I like to go all out because... hell, even demons enjoy gluttonous helpings of food. You can't be a demon without sinning from time to time, I think with a chuckle.

I finally have breakfast made and I decide to go over. I'm actually a little nervous which is really unusual for me, but I also know how she feels about me. Other than her vulnerability last night, we have never really had a civilized conversation. After we eat breakfast though I might have to kick a puppy or something because this weird... warmth I feel inside has got to go.

I knock on the door and at first I don't hear any signs of life. I knock again, this time louder. She opens the door a little and peeks outside. I can see the sleepiness in her eyes and I realize I might have woken her up.

"I'm sorry if I_"

"No it's okay, I was awake." she says cutting me off. She scrutinizes me before raising her brow. "Is that breakfast?" she says as she looks at the two plates I'm holding in my hands. Than for the first time ever she smiles at me and opens the door taking the plate with the most food on it out of my hands.

"That was mine." I say with a smile.

"It tastes better if it's stolen." She's looking over her shoulder as she saunters to her kitchen. I follow her and she sits down at the table that's there. I pull out the chair and sit down awkwardly not really knowing what to say. Luckily she breaks the silence first. "So, to what do I owe the pleasure?" she asks right before stuffing a forkful of eggs into her mouth. I look around at the kitchen and it's really clean. The counters are shell white and the cupboards are light brown, the floors are a tile with the mix of the two. I look back into her beautiful blue eyes.

"I thought you seemed off last night and might want a nice breakfast." I know I probably shouldn't have pointed out her vulnerability, but it's the truth. Wow the truth, it doesn't taste as awful as I thought it would. I see a dark shadow cross her face and for a second I think she is going to tell me to leave.

"This breakfast is delicious, thank you." Then she gets up and walks toward a full pot of coffee. "Would you like a cup of coffee while I'm making one for myself?"

"Most definitely." That was what I was lacking this morning. I got so distracted with making breakfast I forgot about the caffeine. She brings back two cups.

"I hope you like cream and sugar because I didn't think to ask." She hands me the cup.

"I don't really care what's in it as long as there is coffee." I take it from her. She squints her eyes as she studies me.

"There's something different about you this morning." I feel exposed by her... and not in the way I have been working fruitlessly to achieve either.

"I don't think so, if it makes you feel any better I could come over there and grope you." I give her a sly grin that I hope is hiding this sudden vulnerability that has recently enveloped me.

She shakes her head feigning disgust which is impressive because up until now it was real disgust. I guess I'm finally upgrading. "Don't push it." Her smile softens which I have never been the recipient of. "Thank you for the breakfast." Suddenly I feel something else I'm not prone to. Something so foreign I don't even know what it is, but I think I like it.

I know I shouldn't say anything because it's probably going to create tension, but I need to know. "So about this letter..." and I leave the rest unsaid because I'm pretty sure she knows how the sentence will finish. She freezes mid bite and slowly looks up at me and I see something akin to fear in her eyes.

"It's from an ex of mine. I really don't want to talk about it." I feel jealous, but I don't really know why because she obviously doesn't want anything do with him if she fears him. Then I feel anger because who is this man who would strike fear into this fearless woman.

"Does he want to get back together?" I ask with clench fists.

She laughs at that, but there is a cold edge to it. "Maybe, but more than likely he wants to see me dead." The thought of anyone wanting to hurt this lovely creature nearly destroys me.

"Why would that be?" I ask forgetting about the rest of my breakfast.

"Because some men have an issue when their fiancé leaves them at the altar." I'm shocked by this.

"You were engaged?" What's with the jealousy? The thought that she loved someone else is too much.

She rolls her eyes at me. "Yes, and we were blissfully happy." It was my turn to freeze, but when I look at her she has a sarcastic smile. "Obviously."

"So why did you run away?"

"Because the boy who I cared about grew into a man I loathe. Let's just leave it at that." I know she is done with this line of conversation. Honestly I'm surprised she even opened up to me this much. Maybe it's because she helped me or maybe it's because I know she isn't from this world, but either way it's refreshing.

"So..." she starts and I look up at her. "What's up with you anyways?" I look at her confused. "You seem to have your fair share of secrets, unless you having me run around messing with the minds of the townspeople was a ploy." I can tell she's waiting for an answer.

"Let's just say that like you I am different from the human race." I really don't want to go into it any further.

"And?" she isn't going to let it go.

"And... like you I have my own powers and also my own secrets." I hope this time she gets the point.

"Ah, I see, if I show you mine you'll show me yours right?" Suddenly I'm intrigued.

"I like where this is going." My eyes rove over her.

She just rolls her eyes again. I wonder if she does that often or just when we speak. "I meant about who and what we are."

"Oh!" I'm only slightly disappointed. "Alright you go first." To that she shakes her head.

"Not now." I want to call her a tease... a double tease actually. "I guess we should have a little mystery between us." She has a mischievous smile.

I finish up my forgotten breakfast and we talk about lighter things and it is so easy. I don't know what this means, but I hope that it means that I can move in a little closer to her. Then she says "This was really nice." and smiles at me. It's beautiful moment until I remember who I am and nice is not something I do. I am a demon, not nice. I glare at her, get up and walk out of the house without looking back.

I GO TO MY CLUB TO meet up with some of the other demons. There is always a few of them hanging out there because there is nowhere else for them to really go. When I get there I order a drink because, who cares if it's before noon here. I'm from hell.

"I saw Angus today." One of the demons mentions to me.

"Oh yeah?" is my reply.

"He has turned into something about as scary as a declawed kitten. We have to kill that bitch for doing this to him." I feel the need to strike this demon I barely even know.

"And how do you suppose we do that?" I keep my voice cool.

"Have you seen her soul? Imagine the power we could have if one of us were able to devour it. I'm itching to own it myself, not to mention how fucking hot she is." My fists tighten. "I mean seriously, I bet she's an animal in the sack." Why won't he just shut the hell up? Finally I turn to him.

"Stay away from her." I snarl and his eyes widen.

"I-I just meant that we could take our revenge and gain power. Isn't that what you want for our growing army?" He is nervous now. I see a gleam of sweat on his forehead. I give him a look that says 'move along now while you still can' and he walks over to another group of demons and sits with them.

What has this woman done to me, first she says "this is nice" and now I am defending her to other demons. This is getting seriously out of control.

Chapter Six

(Siren)

All day I keep thinking about how odd my encounter with Daemon was. It's not exactly like him to come by with breakfast although to be fair, I don't know him well enough to assume anything. Then I think of Zeek's kiss, yummy I must admit. That sexy man can definitely kiss that's for sure. Then my mind goes to darker matters, the threatening letter. It can only be from one person. My ex. Why won't he just leave me alone?

After I work for a couple of hours, I go to the shelter to keep my mind off the three men in my life. Annabelle is there and as we make the meal and serve the homeless we get chatting more. I really like her, she's sweet.

After the dishes are cleaned up, the other volunteers and I are walking out the door.

"Hey Anna, would you like to go to a club with me tonight?" I hope she says yes because I really need to let loose and forget my troubles for a few hours.

She smiles at me, "Sounds like fun." and we make our way over. It's within walking distance, only a few blocks away. Neither of us are dressed up but at least we don't look like we have been slumming it either.

I know this isn't the best neighbourhood so I keep an eye out because I don't want this human to get into trouble. We get in there and order our drinks and immediately she drags me onto the dance floor. I see a few men leering at us, they better think twice about approaching my new friend.

It isn't long before a man approaches me from behind and he wraps his arms around my waist and is dancing unwisely close to me. He whispers in my ear, "You are going to pay for what you did to Angus you stupid bitch".

I turn my head and smile at him and thankfully Anna is none the wiser to this interaction. "Threatening me shows very poor judgement on your part."

He eyes Anna and says, "I wonder what your friend will sound like screaming as I kill her." That is more than I need to hear. I turn around and catch the man off guard as I slide my lips over his and breathe magic into his mouth. My breath entering his mouth is ice cold. He stumbles back holding his throat. "What did you do to me?" I smile and give him a little wave as he leaves, with the knowledge that he will turn into ice. With the warm temperatures, he will than turn into water. Oops.

I feel someone glaring at me and look over to see Daemon. He is of course talking to a sexy blonde who is also glaring over at me. I turn away from him and his next conquest. I continue to dance with Anna. We are havening a great time regardless of the glares I get from Daemon and some of the other patrons.

I am dancing when I feel someone dancing behind me and he runs his hands down my arms. I turn around to push whoever is brave enough to touch me away, when I turn and see familiar green and gold eyes. "You look amazing!" He puts his arms around me and pulls me close to him.

"Thanks, you don't look to bad yourself." as I wrap my arms around his neck. We dance like that, and for a man who radiates holiness he dances like sin. He bends his head towards mine and takes my lips in a searing kiss. I kiss him back, but before I even know what is happening he is ripped away from me and Daemon is punching him in the face.

"Get away from her you fucking Angel!" and I have no idea what is going on. I just watch them as they fight.

"What do you care Daemon?" The way he says his name is full of a loathing. "You think something as despicable as you has any chance with such a woman?" Things continue to escalate. I look over at Anna and she is looking on in shocked surprise.

Finally I have had enough of this cock fight and walk over to them and push them away from each other using a little magic to pry them apart. I stand in between them.

"What is wrong with the pair of you?" They both glare at the other. "Whatever, you can kill each other if you want too." I turn back to Anna and pull her with me, away from those two men and we continue to dance on the other side of the room.

"What was that about?" she asks me.

"I don't know. One is my neighbour and the other is a man I have gone on a couple dates with." and then she gives me a knowing smile.

"Seems to me that maybe your neighbour might be jealous than." She looks at the men who are talking to each other and even though the hostility is coming off them in waves, they are at least done pummeling each other. "Damn, those two are definitely sexiness incarnate." Then she looks back at me. "You are a very lucky girl."

I smile at her. "Let's just dance and forget about them." and that is what we do. We dance, letting the music pour over us. I look over at Daemon and he is talking to the blonde again, occasionally looking over at me. For some reason it bothers me, but I try to push down those feelings. Why should I care? I look around for Zeek, but he seems to have disappeared as quickly as he appeared.

At the end of the night, I walk Anna to her car and then continue on my way home. As I get back, I look at the door next to mine and consider going up there. Before I can change my mind, I walk up to the door and knock. When the door opens, who I see isn't the man I was looking for but the woman who he was talking to.

She smiles at me and purrs, "Sorry, Daemon is a little busy at the moment." and she closes the door in my face. Nice.

I go back to my house and for some reason his rendezvous bothers me more than normal. Yuck, he's a whore, I should definitely get over whatever this ugly emotion is I'm feeling. Sure I saw a different side of him this morning but what about all the other times. What about him threatening me in order to get what he wanted from me. He isn't anyone I want to associate with.

I walk into my bedroom and see a bouquet of wilted roses with another note. This one is just a simple message.

Hope you enjoyed tonight because soon you will be mine.

I hold the note in my hands trying not to shake. Shit, shit, shit, what am I going to do? He isn't going to stop until he gets me back.

I hear a knock on the door and jump before eyeing the door with suspicion. Let's be honest here, a man who would leave notes in my room isn't going to knock on the damn door. I take a deep breath to calm my nerves and slowly walk to the door and open it up. On the other side is Zeek and he looks pissed.

"What the hell is going on between you and Daemon?" As he yells there is bits of spittle flying from his mouth.

"Nothing is going on between us I swear, I think friends might be too strong a word." and he pushes his way into my home.

"You were doing his bidding and now he is acting like a jealous boyfriend? I highly doubt nothing is going on between you." I look at his huge frame and notice his shadow behind him, the one with ginormous wings protruding from the shadow figures back. "What are you?" he snarls at me.

I look back at his face. "What are you?" and then I remember what Daemon called him. "Oh my Go... gosh, you're an angel aren't you?" He doesn't react at all. "You have been spying on me haven't you?" Again nothing but rage is coming from him.

"I will ask you again, what is going on between you two?" Then he brandishes a sword of white light.

"What? Are you going to kill me?" I laugh at the thought.

"You kill without remorse like much of the evil in this town." At that I laugh harder, darker.

"You're an angel, don't you kill in order to do your job?" I cross my arms over my chest. "Do you feel remorse?"

"That's different!" he spats.

"Why, because you do it in the name of some holiness? Not once have I killed an innocent, so how is it different?"

"Because you do it in the name of evil?"

I laugh at that, "Evil? I kill evil to eradicate it the same as you do. I save innocents the same as you do. How am I any more evil than you are?" My tone becomes harsh. "Unlike you, I don't consider myself as some kind of greatness, I know I'm not."

"Everything I do is for the greater good!"

"Yes and I am just some evil scum I suppose?" I walk toward him. There is no way I am letting him threaten me. "Why do I have to be either good or evil?" I put my face in his face. "Maybe I just am! Now get out of my home." I look down at the sword, "And you better never use that to threaten me again." With a little magic, I manipulate the air around him and push him out the door, the door slams behind him. Damn, I liked him a little.

(DAEMON)

After seeing Siren kissing both of those two men tonight I am willing to take Gwen up on her offer. I take her back to my house where I hope I can forget all about Siren inside my old lover. I just want to forget about that mind consuming woman. We are kissing and it's a clashing of tongue and teeth when there is a knock on the door and Gwen smiles and says "I'll get if for you, I'll be back." She opens the door and shit, its Siren and I hear Gwen talk to her and then shut the door, knowing it was in her face.

"What was that for?" I ask angrily.

"What?" her tone is faux innocence. "It was your neighbour, I just told her you were busy." She reaches for the button of my pants and I push her hands away from me.

"Get out!" She looks up at me with shock.

"But, don't you want me to finish things?" Then her voice lowers to the familiar purr, "I have missed you're body".

"If you don't get out of here I will forcibly remove you, now go!" I yell at her.

She turns and walks to the door. "This is because of that neighbour of yours isn't it?" she hisses over her shoulder. "That stupid bitch!" Then she slams the door behind her. I than notice yelling coming from next door and shortly after her door slams too. I rush over to her place to see if she's alright.

Instead of knocking on the door, I burst through the door and she turns with an almost feral look on her face, and then it softens. "What do you want? Shouldn't you be busy with that blonde?" She actually sounds a little jealous.

"What happened in here?" I walk over to her where she is visibly shaken.

"I got another letter and then Zeek came by." She looks at me accusingly. "How do you know an angel?"

Her question throws me off balance. "We go back a long time." is all I am willing to admit for now.

"No, you know him and if you don't want to tell me now then you can get the hell away from me too." She is livid.

I go to her, "Siren..." but she cuts me off.

"I can't deal with you right now so can you please just go home and let me deal with tonight?" I can see she really doesn't want to fight. She looks almost vulnerable.

"Fine." I swallow my desire to go to her. "We will talk about this tomorrow." Before she can object I leave, closing the door behind me.

(EZEKIEL)

I can't believe that I just went over there and blew my cover, I think as I walk back to where I am staying. I threatened and pulled out my sword as if I was going to strike her down. I don't even know if I would have been able to hurt her.

I replay her words in my head. My actions are nothing like hers. She tortures her victims and allows them to die slowly and in agony. At least I do it swiftly. It is true that not one of her victims were innocent, but that doesn't make what she does right.

Then I think about the fact that she volunteers at a shelter. Those are not the actions of evil. This woman is so confusing.

Suddenly I feel a blast of demonic magic hit me square in the chest and I fly backwards into a brick wall in an alley way. I get up.

"Why did you go to her?" Daemon growls and he is furious.

"Why do you care?"

"She belongs to me." He has a weird look on his face like he can't believe that he just said that.

"Does she now? She says you are barely friends." I snarl in a tone I barely recognize as my own.

"Stay away from her." With that he storms off. That was so unlike the demon I have known for many, many millennia. This is the first time I have seen him impassioned about anything other than his own gruesome crimes, and not to forget about sex. Those are the only things that demon has ever cared about.

I remember her lips on mine and how good she tasted, maybe she got under my skin too. Too bad I screwed everything up, there is no way she will ever trust me now.

Chapter Seven

(Siren)

The next morning I decide I have to go and restore my magic, I used quite a bit last night and never did restore it after saving Daemon's ass.

I go to the lake where I can enjoy the tranquility and take a cleansing breath. I take in the nature and absorb it into my body, into my magic and again the land is vibrant and beautiful.

"What are you?" I hear from behind and me. I turn around to see that Daemon's blonde is standing there with an evil smile on her face.

"What do you want?" I say exasperated. I just want to be alone and prepare for a battle that I know is inevitable.

"To rid Daemon of you." She flicks her wrist and something smashes me in the chest. I look down to see nothing. I look back at her with my head tilted to the side trying to figure out what just happened. She looks at me with shock on her face, which than turns to anger as she strikes me again and again. I just stand there and instead of fighting back I give an exaggerated yawn.

"Are you done now?" and her strikes become frantic and now the anger is gone and all I see is fear.

"Why won't you die?" I walk over to her, hold out my hand and hold her in place.

"Because," I whisper right in her face. "I am more powerful than you." I close my lips as if I am going to blow in her face, but suck in a breath instead. I see her chest start to inflate and there is real fear in her face. "I will let you live this time." I release her before she vanishes like she was never there.

Damn, now I have to restore my magic further... women!

I START OFF STORMING back to my place, but I detour to Daemons instead. I knock on the door, turn the knob which was unlocked and walk into his place. He walks over to me like I just woke him up.

"Why did your bimbo try to kill me?" I yell at him.

"Wait? What?" he asks clearly confused.

"You know, blonde hair, hot, and was here last night?" He visibly pales.

"Gwendolyn!" he seethes. "Nothing happened with her last night and she was none too happy about that."

"Apparently. What does that have to do with me?"

He looks at me and sighs. "Never mind. Did she hurt you?" At that I laugh.

"Do I look hurt?"

He eyes me up and down with his eyes lingering in some place more than others. "No, you definitely don't look hurt, you look sexy." Then his eyes meet my face, "and angry." he gulps. "Is she alive?" he asks.

"Yes, but she won't be if she tries that shit again."

"I don't blame you." He doesn't even seem angry that I just threatened one of his women.

"Aren't you the least bit protective of her?" I can't help but ask.

"At one time, but not anymore." I hate that he has history with her.

"How do you know her?" I know I probably seem jealous and by the smirk on his face, I sound it too.

"Let's just say that we have a long history, but I haven't seen her in two centuries, until last night." I don't know what to make of that.

"Oh!" Man that was smooth.

"Yeah, she and I are old news." He states that with a comforting finality.

(GWENDOLYN)

That bitch had a shit ton of power. What am I going to do? I don't think I am strong enough to kill her. I pace my hotel room not too far from Daemon's place. I want him back and the only way that will happen is to get rid of her.

I feel a powerful essence behind me that materialized out of nowhere. A deep masculine voice like music to my ears says, "I might be able to solve your problem". I slowly turn around to see a man there who is much taller than six feet and his skin is so pale it shimmers. He has short black wavy hair.

"How do you suppose we do that handsome?" He walks over to me.

"Help me weaken Siren and I will do the rest." he says with a smile.

"What is it about this bitch? Does she have a magic vagina?"

He smirks at that. "She has a magical everything, but no matter how powerful she is, her magic pales compared to mine." He looks me up and down with lust.

"How do you suppose I weaken her? She will never allow me near her after today?"

He hands me a vile of glowing thick liquid. "Drink this right before you fight her, you don't need much." He is checking me out. "It will make you impervious to her magic." He walks over to me, "Do not kill her understand? If you do, I will kill you." and with that he is gone.

I look down at the liquid, "Game on".

That night I go to her house and wait for her to come home, relaxing and waiting to strike. Soon I will get her away from Daemon and I will get him back.

With my dark magic I turn off her electricity and then I appear in her home. I strike her with my magic, catching her off guard as she stumbles into a wall.

(SIREN)

I turn around after being hit by magic and see no one other than Gwendolyn. I smile a feral smile and strike at her, but nothing happens. I march toward her and push her into the wall and try to suck in her breath. Nothing. She strikes me again and I fall to the ground. She than punches me with a continuous rhythm until I kick her feet from under her.

I get up quickly and rush for the kitchen, but she strikes me from behind. I finally make it and grab a knife from the chopping block and slice my hand open. I let Gwendolyn get close to me and then I slap her across the face with my bloodied hand. Nothing.

She smiles at me and uses her magic to throw me like a rag doll and I can feel my magic weakening with every strike. I throw magic at her as a defence, over and over again and she doesn't even flinch.

"Why are you doing this?" I say huffing and puffing on my hands and knees.

"Because you have something I want." She then kicks me in the stomach.

"Hello Siren." a familiar voice says from behind me. "Miss me my love?" That term of endearment makes me want to be sick.

I turn to look at him as I slowly get up. I try to hide the fear I feel. Ropes of magic come from his hands and wrap around my wrists obliterating every ounce of my magic for the time being, including my disguise. I feel the tears streaming down my face as I know there is no way I can get out of this. He is the only being I have ever met who is more powerful than I am.

The door bursts open and Daemon is there. "What the hell is going on?" He looks at me with no recognition. "Who are you people?" than he looks at Gwendolyn, "Where is Siren?"

(DAEMON)

I look around the room at the scene before me and I am baffled. I see a man with Black hair and alabaster skin holding a being with the same skin colour but hair a dark navy blue and royal blue wings coming from her back with ice blue spread throughout them. She looks over at me with the most beautiful blue eyes I have ever seen, the same blue eyes I fantasize about looking at me with longing. Those eyes have tears streaming from them. Siren?

"Let her go!" I yell as I throw magic at the man holding her. He flinches and then holds me in place with one hand while he holds the laces of magic around Siren's hands with the other. I don't understand why she isn't fighting him. The scarier aspect is that he was powerful enough to subdue her in the first place.

"She is coming home with me where she belongs," and then they are both gone.

I turn to Gwen, "What the hell are you doing here?" I walk over to her and she backs away from me until her back hits the wall.

"I was saving you from her." she says with uncertainty. "I did it for us".

"There is no us." I snarl in her face. "Where is he taking her?"

"I don't know." she says. "I was just told to weaken her for him, I don't even know what he plans to do with her."

"If I were you Gwen, I would hide because the next time I see you, I will not be accountable for my actions." She then vanishes with a little sob.

I may not know what Siren is or where she was taken, but I am going to find out. I am not going to lie though, she looked an awful lot like a faerie. Those don't exist do they?

(SIREN)

Immediately we land in a beautiful room. The walls are an amethyst purple and the curtains and bed sheets are both a much lighter shade of the same colour and a king sized bed with drapes around it. I don't struggle, without my magic it would be a lost cause.

"Siren, I want you to be comfortable. I want us to get married and rule this powerful kingdom. Between the two of us, with how strong our magic is, we could bring other kingdoms to their knees."

"What if I don't want that?" I ask while looking him directly in the eyes.

"I am going to try to change your mind."

"You think you can do that with me all tied up?"

"I will wine and dine you." he says as he walks over to a bottle of wine that is on the table in the corner of the room. I must say, it's a nice setup he has here. It's almost like a little apartment. Almost.

"You remembered my favourite kind." I notice as I walk over to him. With his magic, he made it so my hands were no longer bound together, but still there is a lace of magic that is like manacles on my wrists to bind my magic.

"I did, I wanted to show you that I remember all the moments we had before everything fell apart." he pours me a glass. He doesn't pour himself one.

"Don't you want one?" I ask pointing at the wine bottle.

"No, I best keep a clear head." He sits in one of the chairs, and I do the same. I take a sip of the decadent wine. The fruits and berries we have are different than the ones in the human world. These ones, when fermented, would make moonshine look like water if they were to drink this wine. I take a sip and let the liquid roll around on my tongue before letting it slide down my throat as he watches me with interest.

"You're loss." I say as I take a bigger gulp.

"Hardly." he mutters under his breath and then louder says, "So, did you enjoy the magicless world?"

"Very much." I put the glass back down on the table. "They are very entertaining."

"I don't know why you would rather be there when you can live here with me."

"Vulcan, you care too much for power." I look pointedly at my wrists. "Apparently you have no qualms of binding mine."

"I just want you to see we could be happy together."

"I really, highly doubt that." He gets up to leave the room.

"Well I will give you time to consider this opportunity."

"Well, when you say it so eloquently, why the hell not?" I spit sarcastically.

Chapter Eight

(Daemon)

I rush from Siren's house to seek out Ezekiel. I don't know if he will help me or not but I can tell that regardless of what he might admit, he does on some level care for Siren.

I end up finding him on a huge hill just outside of town. It's peaceful at this time of night.

"What do you want?" Ezekiel asks on a sigh.

"It's Siren. She was taken by some weird looking guy." I play out the scene in my head in disbelief. "Siren looked so different too. Pale skin, dark blue hai and beautiful blue wings." I know as I am telling him this, I probably sound like I'm in a daze. "She looked like a...a... faerie!"

To that he turns around. "A faerie?" he asks with the same disbelief in his tone as I feel.

"Do they even exist?" I ask him.

"I don't know. I have heard things. Some of the higher ups have wanted to capture one for it is rumoured that their tears can eliminate evil. They wanted to use them on your kind." He says shaking his head.

"Huh." I think about the time I saw her crying and how I touched her tear. I touched her tear! Since then I have been feeling... different! "Shit! That explains it."

"Explains what?" Ezekiel raises an eyebrow.

"Nothing, forget it. We need to get Siren back."

"She's better off where ever she is."

"I am going to get her back. Are you going to help me or not?" I have no more patience for any of this.

"No." is all he says back.

DEMONS AND ANGELS HAVE a trick that we rarely ever use. We can get inside the mind. Demons find it more fun to manipulate our victims to do things they actually want to do but can't due to societal norms.

I relax my subconscious and focus on Siren. I focus and concentrate, but nothing happens. I can't find her. I have to remember that she isn't in this world anymore. Her abductor probably took her back to where ever they are from.

With that in mind, I close my eyes and try to connect with her. I have stalked her, had tried to get my bearings on her and now hopefully it will all pay off. I focus on the blonde girl I originally met with devastatingly cobalt eyes. The same blue eyes she had when in her faerie form with navy hair and alabaster skin that appeared as if almost glowing. I focus on her power, the way she tortures and the way she cares about innocent lives. The way she looked at me when she wanted to kill me and even more importantly, how she looked at me when I brought her breakfast. That look warmed my insides unlike the scathing ones.

Finally I catch hold of something. I'm not sure if it's her because it's too fuzzy.

"Siren?" I call out.

"Daemon?" I hear. Her form becomes clearer as I stare at her.

"Where are we?" I say as I look around. I notice she is in a bedroom. "Are you sleeping?"

"We are in the room where I am currently being held captive, until I submit and become the faerie queen." She looks around the room. "No, I'm not sleeping, but I am a little drunk from the wine King Vulcan left for me."

I laugh "Vulcan? What kind of name is that?"

"I think it's safe to say neither of us can throw stones at glass houses, don't you think Demon?"

"Fine." he says on a sigh.

"How are you inside my head Daemon?" She gives me a weary look. "Now you have seen mine, it's time for me to see yours."

"I'm a demon." To this she cracks up with laughter. "What?"

"You're a demon and your name is Demon?"

"I pronounce it Damon!" he growls at me. "Now, I want to come and get you." he says. "But I don't know how to."

"I don't know how you can get here." she has been clearly thinking of ways. "Wait, I got it." She smiles. "Go to my apartment and look for sparkling dust."

"Siren, is this really the time to ask me to clean your apartment?"

"Shush and listen! The dust is faerie dust..."

"Can I use it to fly if I only believe?" he jests, cutting me off.

"Listen closely Peter Pan. Now, I want you to sprinkle it on yourself and think of me when you do it. You got inside my head so this should be no great feat."

"Okay, I can do this, but can I ask you a serious question?"

"Sure."

"What happens if I say I don't believe in faeries?"

"I'll slap you upside the head is what will happen if you say that?" she threatens.

"So you won't die?" I ask.

"I won't, but you might. I am no Tinkerbell and you are most definitely not Peter Pan."

"Okay, alright, I get it. So I sprinkle this non-flying faerie dust on myself and focus on you."

"That's right."

"I got this Siren. I am going to come and get you."

(SIREN)

I slept like the dead last night. It could have been my over indulgence in fine wine or it could have been the most comfortable bed I have ever slept in. I guess we'll never really know.

I wake up to a knock on the door. I sit up in bed as a man comes in with a cart of food that looks and smells delicious. With it is some juice. The man takes the cart and wheels it over to me so my food is sitting in front of me like a table. I have never been made breakfast in bed, but I wasn't going to argue about the opportunity to have one now.

"Thank you." I give him an eager smile, all but licking my chops. I dove right into it and I probably looked like a savaged animal.

When I was done, Vulcan came in and sat on the side of the bed. "Wow, you must have been hungry."

"Starving. It was so good, I almost choked a couple times while shovelling it all in."

"I'm glad it was up to your standards, after all you will be my wife." He gives me a smile.

"Let's not get ahead of ourselves here. I am still not convinced this is for the best." I try to ignore the gut wrenching feeling that comes with the thought of becoming his queen.

"How did you sleep my lovely Siren?" His smile looks sincere which brings back memories of the boy I fell in love with, rather than the man I could live without seeing again.

"I slept well thank you." I try to smile as sincerely back, but I feel it might have fallen short.

"I'm glad to hear that." He then turns to walk out of the room. "Oh yes, I almost forgot. Siren, there will be a dress delivered to you today. There will be a ball tonight in honour of the queen they thought they lost. I want you to look your best." With that he walked out the bedroom door.

I GO TO THE BALL WITH Vulcan by my side in a shimmering royal blue dress that is similar to the colour of my wings which are hidden in my back. As we descend the steps hand in hand, I watch as a room full of people slowly turn to look at us. Written on some of their faces is the displeasure I expected to see. On others I see sheer joy at my return. There was one face in particular that seemed absolutely morose. My sister Cassandra is looking on, and I know she wished for things to be better for me. I try to give her a wide smile in order to tell her everything is going to be okay but when she smiles back, hers only says 'I truly hope so.'

"Would you like to have this dance?" Vulcan asks me as he wraps his arms around my waste.

I look into his face and wrap my arms around his neck "Yes you may."

I try to play the part of the doting fiancé, but it just doesn't feel right to me because this is not the man I want to be seeing. I really hope Daemon can get some faerie dust so that he can rescue me sooner rather than later. Until then I have to play the part.

He holds me close as we dance, and before I know it he is adding some twirls to the mix. "I missed you Siren." he says as he leans in to give me a kiss. I close my eyes and kiss him back, just a peck, but one I would rather not have received. A throat clearing interrupts us.

"Siren, we must catch up." I turn to see Cassandra with a big fake smile plastered onto her face. She pulls me in for a hug and then grabs my arm to pull me toward one of the tables to sit down. "Are you really going to marry him?" she asks me once no one is around.

"I am really hoping not to." I admit. "I have someone who is trying to rescue me if he can find my faerie dust."

She shakes her head at me. "Really, be serious now."

"There really is someone. My neighbour at home actually." She raises her eyebrow at me. "Yes, it has become my home. He is a demon evidently and says he will rescue me. If not I guess I am marrying Vulcan."

"You will not!" she smiles. "I know you well enough to know that you will never do anything you don't want to." That makes me smile.

"You're right, so I'm really hoping plan A works because plan B is going to be a bitch."

"What is plan B?" she asks.

"I don't know. That's why it will be a bitch."

"Okay. What about this demon?" she asks me.

"I don't know, he's my neighbour. He's pretty good looking and up until a day or two ago, I couldn't stand the sight of him. There is something sweet under all the whoring and trouble making." I tell her with a slight smile.

"Oh does someone like him?" she asks coyly. Her smile fades. "I don't know anything about demons because I kind of assumed they were a myth." She is staring at her fingers as she drums them on the table. "Aren't they supposed to be evil?"

"Probably. He definitely has his moments." I think back to when he forced me to mess with the minds of the people in town. "He is evil."

"Then why are you trusting him to save you?" Now that is a very good question.

"Because he made the effort to contact me through a dream." At her puzzled look I say, "Must be a demon thing."

I see a look cross her features that could only mean trouble. "I could find him and bring him here for you".

"I don't know if that's a very good idea."

"Why not? I could bring him and he could free you." She sounds overjoyed by the idea.

"What if you get caught?" I reprimand her.

"What if I don't?" I know there is nothing I can say that will change her mind now.

"Fine, but if you end up getting caught and being punished to death, I will kill you myself." She grins at me a sinful grin.

"I'll leave tonight."

Vulcan walks over to me with an outstretched hand and I take it before looking back at my frowning sister who just gives a slight nod.

I go off and dance. For hours I am either dancing or conversing with those I haven't seen in a few years.

IT'S NEARING THE END of the night when Vulcan whispers in my ear "Ready for bed my sweet?"

"Yes, I am exhausted." I stumble a bit as we walk away.

"Did you over indulge in the alcohol?" he eyes me as he helps me walk to my bedroom.

I giggle. "Maybe a little."

He walks me to my room and lies me in my bed. Before he leaves he kisses me on the lips and then inhales a few solid breaths. I feel a weird buzzing throughout by body. Damn that must have been some good alcohol

***.

(Daemon)

I go through Sirens things trying to find this 'dust' that she was telling me about. I was sure it was going to be in her underwear drawer. I went through all the little sexy garments that I would love to see her in to no avail, but alas, there was no faerie dust in there. I went through every one though. Thongs and bikini style made from lace and silk, while picturing her in every single piece. All I got out of that was an erection.

I went through her closet looking through her clothes. Dresses, blouses, shorts, halter tops, short and long skirts and pants. Some were scantily clad which left little to the imagination. Why have I never seen her wearing most of these things? Other than when she came to my club, I have never seen her in anything like what I found in here. Still no dust.

I move on to the less enticing objects, like under couch cushions all the way down to the fibres of the rugs and floor mats. I did find little bits of shimmering dust, but when I tried to get to her, it apparently wasn't a sufficient amount.

I am trying to collect as much as I can when I hear something fall to the ground and shatter in the living room and a muttered curse. I run out hoping to see Siren, but instead, I see a beautiful woman with red hair as if it was spray painted on, and wings of similar colour.

"Who the hell are you?" I ask her.

"Hello, you must be Daemon, the demon who is to help my sister." she says with the kind of smile I have seen on many women's faces before. "She must have forgotten to mention how gorgeous you were." She is eyeing me up and down when she gets to my eyes. "Sorry for my rudeness. I'm Cassandra, Sirens sister, and I am here to take you to her, although, I am having second thoughts". Her smile turns friendlier when she says "What a lucky girl she is".

"You are going to bring me to her?"

"Yes, before she has to marry Vulcan." She says the name with distain.

"Are you going to bring me right to her?" I ask skeptically.

"Yes, that is the plan, although we are going to have to wait until morning, so you might as well go home and get some rest so we can leave early."

"I am just next door." I say as I walk out of Siren's place.

I am so happy that I finally cut a break here. I don't know if I ever would have gotten enough faerie dust to save her otherwise. I definitely have to get to her before she has to marry this Vulcan dude. No way is she going to marry some other guy before I get a chance to have her.

Chapter Nine

(Siren)

I wake up to Vulcan coming into my room. He is wearing an arrogant smile and a dark grey suit that makes his skin look pale, but accentuates his dark hair and eyes. "Time to take these manacles off you." he says with a wave of his hand.

I instantly try to use my magic to get out of there but nothing happens. I try again and still nothing. His smile grows wider and smugger. "Is your magic not working?" The way he says it reminds me of the man I left behind.

"What did you do to me?" I ask with vehemence.

"That wine I gave you was your favourite right? I bet you drank the whole bottle didn't you?" I feel nauseated and I glare at him so he continues. "It's funny that all you need is a drop of basilisk venom in a bottle of wine to be consumed. It started shutting things down slowly." I feel myself pale. Shit! "It was pretty easy to steal your magic once the poison was in your system."

"How could you do this to me? Were you just pretending to be the man I loved so long ago?" I ask. "How could you poison me?"

He laughs and it's tainted with malicious intent. "Did you really think I was going to let some stupid little faerie jilt me?" and he stomps over to me, tilts my head up so I can look him in the eyes. "You will now get what you deserve." With that he turns around and walks out of the room throwing over his shoulder "You can leave now that I have your magic."

I feel a kind of helplessness I have never felt in my life. I knew he would betray me sooner or later, but poison me? Not just poison me, but to do so with one of the worse poisons known to us? It's only a matter of time before I weaken and die. It isn't a quick death.

I stand there in a shocked stupor when two people materialize a few feet in front of me.

"Siren are you alright?" Cassandra runs over to me.

I can feel the tears wanting to come, but I refuse to cry. Instead I say with no inflection, "I'm free to go".

"Just like that he's letting you go?"

I hide my despondence. "Yep, he realized he didn't want me to be his wife after all." It is the truth, but I have no idea how to tell her that I am going to die. The thing about basilisk venom is that there is no known way to stop it, I do however know someone who might know of something that could help. "I need to see Evelyn." That makes Cassandra's eyebrows shoot up.

"Why?" she gasps.

"I think I might need her help" I reply.

"Do you want me to come with you?"

"NO!" I say *too* quickly and far too loudly. A worried look appears on her pretty face. "I just want to ask her for a simple recipe to hide from Vulcan in the future." I also need to find a way to not die. I can't tell her the whole truth though. She will attack Vulcan and die which I cannot allow.

"I better go before anyone sees me." With that she is gone.

"Daemon, can you get us out of here with your demon powers?" I ask him.

He looks at me perplexed. "I think so, but can't you?"

"My magic seems to be on a hiatus." and before he can say anything I add "Just get me out of here".

"Okay." he wraps his arms around me and materializes us outside the palace walls.

"We better start walking to see Evelyn." I tell him.

"Who is she?"

"She's a faerie healer who has many other spells as well."

"You need help with your magic don't you?" he asks me.

"For starters."

WE LOOK AROUND AT THE lush greenery and the vibrant colours. "It's beautiful here" he says.

"It really is. I missed it in the last two years." I walk over to a beautiful bright crimson red flower with light pink on the inside that looks similar to an orchid, but twice as big. I pick it and take a sniff before placing it in my hair.

We start walking when he asks the dreaded question, "So, what happened to your magic?"

I walk over to a few berries and say, "These berries can make some serious alcohol but are delicious all the time." I pick a couple and put them in my mouth.

"I know you are trying to change the topic, but I don't understand why."

"Oh that's an easy one. Because I don't want to talk about it." I continue on ahead of him.

He speed walks to catch up to me. "Fine, I'll let it go." He walks beside me while looking around at everything. "So why did you leave here?"

"Vulcan was a childhood friend of mine. We grew up together and were the best of friends. You see, he was always destined to be a king, but back then that didn't matter so much." I look away from him. "We fell in love when we were what humans call teenagers, but life had other plans. For the next one hundred and twenty years he was sewing all his wild oats and then some. Eventually he decided he needed a queen and I was the lucky chosen one." I look over at Daemon who is watching. "The rest is history."

"So you left because you didn't want to marry him?" he asks me. "That seems a little drastic."

"No, I was pretty much exiled by my community, friends and family alike, so I ran." I shrug. My foot catches on a rock and I stumble before landing on my hands and knees on more rocks.

"Are you alright?" Daemon asks me. I look at my hands and knees, and they are both skinned. My hand is bleeding a little, but my knee is pretty much an open wound.

"That has never happened to me before." I say looking at the ground and avoiding eye contact with Daemon.

"Never?" he asks me.

"Not since I was a child and didn't know how to use my magic and my wings, both have saved me multiple times." I look at my hand which has small abrasions that heal pretty quickly. I look at my knee and it looks like it's trying to heal, closing and opening again. Finally it heals as well.

"Shouldn't you have healed much faster than that?" he points to my knee.

"Yeah, I'm a little off today." I wave if off with my hand. The poison is working much faster than anticipated. At least I am still healing so there is always that.

WE WALK FOR HOURS AND hours when we come to a cave in the side of a rock hill. "Are you ready to rough it?" I ask him.

"I was born ready." he says with a wink and a smile.

"I can't go on tonight and I don't know how long it will take before we come to another place we can sleep in." I mumble, "I never had to walk it before." He looks over at me with a quirked eyebrow but doesn't say anything.

We walk into the cave which is dark and dank. "Do you have a light?" I ask him.

"Nope!" is all he says. Okay, so this isn't going to be as easy as I would like it to be. All of a sudden I see fire come from his hands and there is a controlled flame in his palm. I look over at him with narrowed eyes.

"What?" he says with a smile. "I said I didn't have a light, I never said I didn't have anything that could make light." He starts collecting debris from around the cave and piling it. He takes the flame that is already in his hand and makes it grow. He holds his hand out and an inferno shoots toward the pile causing a huge camp fire. I look on with awe.

"Wow, that's a cool gift!"

"All part of being who I am." He says with a lopsided smile. He has a boyish look and I can't help but smile back at him. I sit down on the cave ground, which is mostly cushioned with dirt, and enjoy the fire. I stare at the flames, becoming hypnotized when he sits down next to me. He is so close I can feel his arm brush mine. I look over at him and he is watching me.

"Thank you" I say simply and he looks at me perplexed. "For coming for me and for lighting this fire. I don't know what I would have done if I was alone." I think about the alternative and all I see is me alone in the dark. He might not always have been great company, but for whatever reason he decided to be my companion in my world.

"What made you look for me?" I ask without thinking.

"Why wouldn't I?" he takes my hand in his. His hand is warm from holding the fire, but not in any extreme way. "I haven't gotten into your pants yet." To that, I roll my eyes and he grins, but I don't take back my hand. It's nice not being alone when I am in a situation where I feel so lonely.

"Well I might need to hold off on that then because I might need you to save my ass again."

"Oh Siren. I kind of like having you around."

"Well Daemon, I don't mind having you around either. Like fungus, over time you grew on me." I say with a smile to show my humour.

"I've been called worse." he says with a shrug.

"I bet you have."

(DAEMON)

I wake up to the sound of chattering teeth from beside me. I open my eyes and there is Siren curled up in a ball while shivering. I scoot closer to her and then wrap my arms around her pulling her into my chest. It isn't that cold in the cave, especially with the fire, but as I hold her close I notice her skin is freezing. Within a few minutes she stops shivering, sighs and then her breathing evens out. I notice the enticing smell of her and that there is only a couple layers of clothes between us. I wonder if she is wearing any of those sexy underwear I saw in her drawer. I push those thoughts aside and fall back to sleep.

I wake up wound up in a warm body. At some point during the night, Siren all but crawled on top of me. Her head is on my chest and I can feel her breaths against it. I glide my hands lightly up and down her back relishing in the feel of her. I have waited for a moment to sleep with her, I was just hoping that wouldn't be all we did. Well, we have a few more nights for me to seduce her, but right now I am just going to enjoy the feel of her body against mine.

She starts to stir and then looks up at me with sleepy eyes. I smile down at her and she wipes the drool from around her mouth. "Sorry, I didn't mean to use you as a pillow."

"Trust me, I didn't mind it in the least." I murmur as I pull her closer.

"Thank you for warming me up." she whispers. "I have never felt so cold before." Her face pales as if realizing something, but before I can say anything, it's gone as if it was never there.

"It was my pleasure." I can honestly say as simple as it was, I haven't had a greater one in a while and that is including all the women I have taken home. I can't tell her that though.

"Ugh." She rolls away from me and I immediately feel the loss. "I guess we should get going." I notice there is an urgency that wasn't there a few seconds ago.

"We can just stay here for a few hours." I try to pull her closer but she escapes my clasp.

"We really do have to get to Evelyn. I need to see her quickly." She looks at me sheepishly.

"What's the rush?" I sigh annoyed.

"I-uh-I just need to get things sorted out okay?"

"Okay. Just give me a second here to get my shirt on." I tell her as I pull it over my head.

We head out on our way. I look at Siren and her shimmering skin seems slightly duller. "Are you feeling okay?"

"Yes." She giggles nervously which is so unusual that I don't respond back to her.

We are walking through the forest, when I see trees shaking in a path like pattern. A humongous and angry sounding creature is tearing through the forest. I freeze in my place not sure what in the hell that is, pardon my phrasing.

"What is that?" I ask, while grabbing Siren's arm to stop her in place.

"That would be a cyclops." she states pulling her arm back and continuing on her way.

"Shouldn't we hide somewhere until it's out of our vicinity?" I gasp, stating the obvious.

"Why?" she asks with a raised eyebrow.

"Isn't it going to try to eat us?"

"She scoffs at that. "Not unless you dip yourself in salt and butter and even then, they have standards."

The trees are shaking in our direction, but Siren doesn't look the least bit concerned. Suddenly he breaks through the trees and stops to look down at us.

"Hey Stewart" she says with a smile.

"Well look who we have here." He's smiling back at her. "Where have you been hiding out?" I don't like how he is eyeing her up. No pun intended.

"Well I had to go to the world of the humans." she rolls her eyes. "I don't know how they survive with absolutely no magic." She looks up at Stewart "Or brute strength".

"Sounds rough there Siren." He puts his face closer to hers and when she takes a step back, I get into my defensive stance, but she indiscreetly shakes her head. "You look different, almost... I don't know how to describe it."

She shifts her eyes away from him. "I'm on my way to Evelyn's".

"Why don't you just use your magic?" he asks her.

"I lost my magic" she mutters quietly.

"How is that even possible?" he scoffs. "Isn't there only one way to steal magic from a..."

"Yes!" Siren says, cutting him off and her voice sounds angry and then resigned as she says "There is."

"How?" I ask seriously unnerved by her response, but no one answers me. They just stare at each other for a moment.

"Need a lift?" he asks.

"Um..." and she hesitates before answering.

"You're afraid aren't you?" he asks her.

"I thought you weren't afraid of him Siren." It's my turn to quirk my eyebrow.

"You see, cyclops always seem so hostile because they are constantly running into things." she tells me while Stewart nods along with her. "Because they are giants, people have gotten the wrong idea about them. You see, they have no depth perception, so yeah, I am a little scared." She then turns to the cyclops. "How fast can you get us there and more importantly, do you think we can take the path with the least amount obstacles?"

"If you tell me where we need to go I can fly us there." I tell her.

She turns on me and gasps, "You can fly?"

"Can't you?" I ask her.

"Yeah, but I am too weak to do so now." She sounds so dejected I just want to take her into my arms.

"Sorry Stewart" she says. "I hope to see you again soon though." She walks over to him and pats his leg. "I'm glad I ran into you." She chuckles a little, "and not the other way around".

"Ha... ha... always the comedian." Stewart gives her a warm smile. "I've missed you." Siren looks like she's about to say something when he adds, "I know you have a depth perception joke there, but you can just keep it to yourself." She closes her mouth but smiles up at him. Stewart turns to walk away and runs into tree after tree.

"Good thing we didn't go with him."

"Stewart's pretty great." she says and I feel a twinge of jealousy.

"I didn't like the way he was eyeing you up." She then glares at me. "I mean seriously, did he have to keep such a close eye on you?"

"Oh you're so punny." she rolls her eyes, but proceeds to chuckles.

"Seriously though, I think he might have a thing for you." I tell her.

"He's just a really nice guy Daemon." Her eyes narrow at me, "So you can fly and you didn't tell me that before?"

"I didn't think about it. It has been hundreds of years since I have had too." Looking back I can't believe it has been that long, but it has.

"So you might be a little rusty I take it?"

"I'm sure it's like riding a bike." I state.

"You know the first time I rode one I flew over my handle bars." she declares flatly. "I might have had better luck with Stewart." Now she's mocking me. I let my large wings out and she just stares at me with her jaw open.

"Like something you see?" I waggle my eyebrows at her.

"Wow, they're so big." and those words make my chest puff out.

"Now that's what every man wants to hear. Now come here." She walks over to me and I wrap my arms around her. "Tell me what direction we want, alright?"

"Will do."

The feel of her in my arms again gives me a warm feeling I'm not sure about, and definitely not at all comfortable with. As much as I want to ravage her, which I very much want to do, there is something else I feel with her. Maybe it's serenity. We take off into the air and a rush I haven't felt in what feels like forever overwhelms me. It's thrilling to fly again and to do it with this incredibly intoxicating faerie.

"Go left." she says as she points. "Right there, see?" There is a little building that looks similar to a gingerbread house and I wonder if this is where Hansel and Gretel have been. As we land, a woman comes out with platinum blonde hair and wings with white running through them. She has the same pale shimmering skin that I have learned is a faerie trait.

"Siren?" the woman runs over and hugs her. "Are you alright?"

"I need your help."

We go inside and Siren sits down in a chair, while Evelyn sits down in another. I decide to stand a few feet away.

"What can I help you with?" she asks Siren.

"Um..." Siren pauses and fiddles with the hem of her shirt. "I... uh... well..." Come on Siren just tell her what's wrong. How hard can it be since you did seek her out? "So Vulcan gave me wine and I drank it..." Okay, you can do it Siren. "He put a drop of basilisk venom in it and then stole my magic."

"What?" I growl angry and confused. Venom doesn't sound good and from what I know, basilisks are deadly. At least they are in myth.

Evelyn takes Siren's hand. "When did you drink it?"

"Three nights ago?"

A pained look crosses Evelyn's face. "How are you feeling?"

"Just a little weaker. More tired too."

"You know there is no cure here for this?" To that Siren hangs her head and I realize what they are saying. She's dying.

"I know." she whispers.

"You knew you were dying and you didn't think to, I don't know, tell me?" I seethe as I cross the room to Siren's chair.

"I didn't want to talk about it." A tear starts to slide down her face.

I touch her cheek with the back of my hand. "There has to be something we can do." I look questioningly over at Evelyn.

"The only thing I have ever heard of that can cure any illness is a stream in the Garden of Eden."

"What?" She gasps.

"That place doesn't exist." I snarl. "In my thousands of years alive, I have never once heard of its actual existence."

"It does exist." Evelyn says calmly as if I don't intimidate her at all, which I probably don't.

"Where is it?" Siren asks.

Evelyn's face dims as she answers. "I don't know".

"Then how do you know it's real?" I yell at her.

"It's the only cure that can save her so if you can't believe it's real and find it, then Siren is going to die." Evelyn says just as angrily. "I have no proof it's real, but it's literally the only thing she has."

I look at Siren and a strange emotion rolls through me. It might be regret. Regret that she is going to die before I really get to know her maybe? Regret that I won't be able to bed her? I don't know, but I do know that if she dies, I might never identify the regret I am sure to feel for the rest of eternity. Siren looks at me and I can see so much despair in her eyes, and without thinking, I wrap her in my arms and hold her tight. I realize that her arms are wrapped tightly around me as she rests her head in the crook of my neck. I don't want to let her go. I can't risk losing her, I have to find the Garden of Eden.

"We have to find Ezekiel." I say as I grab her hand and pull her up.

"Is that Zeek?" she asks me.

"Yes, now can you help us get back to the human world?" I ask Evelyn.

She smiles. "I happen to have some faerie dust." She hands over a vile. "Try to use it sparingly, because you might need it to get back."

"You know how to get to Ezekiel right?" I just nod.

She holds my hand, and before you know it we are standing in a room that looks to be an apartment, right behind Ezekiel.

"Shit!" he yells before he realizes it's us.

"We need your help." I declare.

"I told you to leave her." he admonishes me.

"She's dying." That strangely gets his attention.

"What happened?" he demands looking her over.

"My ex-fiancé..."She begins.

"You were engaged?" he interrupts her.

"Yes, and when I broke it off he was none too happy. He hunted me down and finally acted like the man I used to know. He was luring me into a false security so he could poison me with basilisk venom and steal my magic." Ezekiel almost looks stunned.

"She needs to find the Garden of Eden." I add. "Do you know if it even exists?"

"I have never seen it or know of anyone else who has." I see apology in his eyes.

"We were told it's the only thing that can help her." I take Sirens hand and squeeze it. She looks down at our hands in blatant disbelief, as does Ezekiel.

"We will try to figure this out." he looks at Siren. "I really don't want anything to happen to you."

"Thanks." She smiles at him. "I am sorry about everything that happened between us. I hope we can get past it." I feel a little anxious at her words. Does she still want him?

"I think we can." he assures her.

"So what are we going to do?" She looks between the two of us.

"I can go to heaven and ask around, see if anyone knows anything that will help us." Ezekiel tells her.

"We can go to hell together if you want and see what they might know of the place." I hope she will want to come with me rather than Ezekiel.

"I think we can do that demon boy." she says with a smile and I find myself relieved.

Chapter Ten

(Siren)

Daemon takes my hand, and before I can even comprehend what we are doing we are in a hot cave. I look around and I can see flickering of what looks a huge fire. It smells like hot stones and I realize that it must be brimstone I smell. This is exactly what I would have expected Hell to be like. Every inhale I take is heated from the air.

"Now I get the saying 'hotter than hell.'" I look around the cave area. "Wow, no wonder people try to avoid this place."

"Hey now. This is my home." He exclaims, but when I look at him his expression doesn't match his outraged tone.

"Now I get why you are the way you are." I elbow him in the side and he makes an "oomph" sound.

"This place has little to do with that." When I look up at him his expression is guarded.

"Well, I guess we might as well get going" I try to gear the conversation into another direction. "Lead the way."

We walk for about ten minutes when I hear females giggling before I hear them shushing each other.

"Daemon is that you?" A pretty red head says as she comes out of the shadows.

"You came to keep us company I hope." A brunette comes up from behind the red head. They are shameless as they walk over to him and start pawing him all but knocking me out of the way.

"What the hell?" I say looking at them. "I forgot where I was." I mutter to myself.

"Ladies, I'm here for another purpose." Daemon tells them.

"Yeah, he's with me." I surprise myself with my jealousy. I only feel irritated because these bimbos were acting as if I was invisible. Yeah, that's it. He pushes them away and grabs my hand, surprising me and making me feel some weird sensations inside.

"Wow stud. You're here for all of ten minutes and your fan club is already starting to reconvene." I can't help the slight.

"I'm sorry about that." When I look up at him he looks a little ashamed.

"You don't owe me anything." I smile, trying to alleviate the tension.

"No, but I would like it if you didn't just see me as a whore." he mutters almost under his breath.

"That's going to take a while." I can't help but say and I hear him exhale a long breath.

"I am really hoping it won't take that long."

"Well stop sleeping with everything that will say yes and you might get there yet." He laughs but it sounds more like a gasp of air.

"I walked away from them easily enough." he points out.

This is true, he did. "If you can do it again, you might start making some leeway."

"Done!" he says quickly.

"You just want in my pants." I roll my eyes at him.

"That would be a definite bonus." he agrees.

WE WALK THROUGH TUNNELS that are well lit from the lava and the flames coming from it. Even though it's incredibly stifling, it's not as unbearable as one would think being this close to it all. I look around at it in wonder. I mean really, my home land is nothing like this. This is actually the complete opposite of it.

Every once in a while I hear grumbling from something in the shadows. *Somethings*. I shake it off and keep going, after all I do have a big strong man. Well, I have Daemon.

"I need to stop for a second and sit down." I finally say.

"Where do you think we should do that?"

"I will sit on the hard rock ground over there." I point to a small enclave. We sit down on the rock ground and take a moment to breathe.

"What do you think?" he asks me.

"It's hot." For some reason I feel like my opinion actually matters. "It's very different from my place, but nothing like what the human bible says. I mean where are the staked bodies? Where are people trying to crawl out of the flames?"

He smiles devilishly. "That's on the other side."

"Well we must go. I assume it's a tourist attraction then?" He laughs. "Seriously, it's something everyone should see, so I will now encourage bad behaviour." I wink at him.

"Good, it will really help to divvy up the work." He winks at me.

I lean into him, sudden exhaustion hitting me. "Hey, are you okay?" he asks as he puts his arms around me. I lean into him further, realizing how comfortable he is. Who would have thought it?

"I don't know if I can go on right now. I think I might need a nap, is that okay?"

"I think we will be okay for a couple of hours here. The beings down here aren't all bad, I mean some are beyond terrible, so we will try not to stay too long." He holds me tighter. "I have my own place that we can go to for real sleep."

"Mmmm." is all I can get out and then I fall asleep.

I am watching as a young boy is forced to kill a village.

"I don't want to." the boy sobs.

"You will do it or you will be punished, only this time worse than last time." The man says. He looks like the boy's father.

"Why? These people are just sleeping." the poor boy is crying.

"If you don't do it I will hurt someone you love every day until you do."

I wake up and look up at Daemon who looks like he is also napping. The boy looked so much like him. Weird. I rest my head on his shoulder again and fall back to sleep.

(Daemon)

I wake up and look over at Siren as she slumbers with her head on me. She is so painfully beautiful that I don't want to look away. I wish I could just hold her like this forever. I have never in my very long existence thought such a thing, it's weird to think it now. I look closer and her skin looks even less shimmery. I really hope we can find the Garden of Eden before the poison runs its course.

Siren starts to stir and her eyes flutter open and she looks up at me. A slight smile crosses her features and then it's gone as if she is remembering her surroundings. She sits up and stretches. "I really needed that." she says on a yawn.

"Yeah, me too." I can't seem to keep my eyes off her.

"Should we get going?" she asks as she starts getting up.

"Yeah, I guess we better before the scarier creatures down here start to take advantage."

"We wouldn't want that now." she says with a smile.

WE WALK THROUGH MORE caves and I realize how much I have missed this place. Missed my home. I know this place is far from perfect with its hellish creatures and so many demons, but it's also a very honest place. A place full of deception is honest in the sense that you know you will be deceived. Not everyone down here is like that though. There are plenty of beings who just live day to day like everyone everywhere else. Those are the few who are harder to gauge because they are the expectation.

As much as I want Siren to love my home because I'm from here, I also don't want her to get tangled up in anything here either. That's really easy to do when this place was created to be a huge trap. We hear more voices up ahead of us and I try to get Siren to walk behind me.

"What is it?" she asks me.

"I'm not sure yet, but I want to make sure you're protected before we get up there." I say truthfully.

As we get closer, I realize I only hear one voice and they are hidden in shadows all alone. It sounds as if the young woman is admonishing herself for something and the voice sounds so sad.

"Hello there." I call out as we head towards her.

"Don't look at me." she hisses as she turns away. I notice her hair is moving on its own accord and immediately, I know what we have encountered.

"Don't look Siren." I shouted louder than necessary.

When you tell someone not to look, they always have to see why not, which is why I'm sure Siren peeked around my body. "Are you okay?" she asks the gorgon.

"No." Her sadness is heartbreaking, even for me.

"What happened?" Siren tries to get closer, but I put my hand on her shoulder to stop her.

"You do realize she's a gorgon right?"

"I thought they were a myth." she says as I lift my eyebrow up at her.

"Yeah. Good thing there are no fairy tales written about faeries."

"You're a faerie?" the gorgon asks.

"A faerie without her magic, but if that counts, then yes I am."

The gorgon sighs deeply. "I just want to be able to look someone in the eyes without turning them into stone." the girl says morosely.

"Will your tears help her?" Daemon asks.

"How did you know about that?" Siren asks with narrowed eyes.

"Ezekiel said something about it."

"No, they won't work. I am pretty sure that the magic in them still holds, even without my powers, but I don't know for sure. The reason it won't work is because, if myth holds true, gorgons are cursed and I can't reverse that." No matter how much I'm sure she would like to for the sake of this girl.

"Have you ever heard of the Garden of Eden?" I ask her.

"Of course I have." the girl answers clearly offended. "Who hasn't?"

"I mean have you ever heard of its whereabouts?" I ask more clearly.

"Isn't it just an old story?" the girl asks.

"Aren't we?" Daemon says with a smile.

The girl turns slightly so we can see the side of her face. "I don't know if it's true, but I might know of someone who can tell us."

"That would be amazing." Siren sounds hopeful.

"I'm Maddy." the girl says.

"Nice to meet you Maddy. I'm Siren and this is Daemon." she says pointing at me.

"Everyone down here knows of Daemon. He's kind of an icon." I was really hoping Siren wouldn't hear more about this.

"Why is that?" Siren asks, almost as if she knows the answer.

"Well the women who have had him, talk about him like he's the best lover they have ever had. The women who haven't, I'm pretty sure have added him to their to-do list. The men who have fought beside him say he is ruthless on the battlefield and takes no prisoners and the men who haven't, wish they could be him or meet him." Maddy sounds a little excited. "I can now say I have met him."

"Let me guess," Siren chimes in. "You wish you could bed him?"

"Gosh no" Maddy says aghast. "I want true everlasting love. I just know I won't ever have it because of what I am."

"Who is this person who might be able to help Siren?" I ask helpfully, while hoping to change the topic back to the problem at hand and away from my colourful past along with Maddy's.

"His name is Xavier and he is not only a fallen angel, but has become a powerful being down here. With his millions of years, he might have heard something about the garden."

"It's worth a try." I say.

(EZEKIEL)

I go to the heavens asking some of the oldest angels I know if they know about the gardens existence. Every single one of them said that they didn't, that it was a myth, a good story to keep people in line, to persuade people from acting on their desires. Every. Single. One. I really don't know what to do now or who else to ask. How can something so significant not be known to these elderly angels. It doesn't make any sense to me. The only thing I can figure is that they're right, it's just a story.

If it is just a story, why would the healer tell Siren to find it? Unless she wants Siren not to lose hope, but even still she is going to die from the poison. From what I understand, the basilisk venom is one of the strongest poisons in all the realms. At least that's what I was told.

There is a very good chance that Siren is going to die and there is nothing we can do about it. I know I considered killing her because I thought she was something evil, but now that she is dying, I regret those callus thoughts. I know she isn't really any different than I am when it comes to eradicating the world of evil. I guess our reasons are different to some degree, but the end result is the same. I am now at the local watering hole where angels come to unwind after a job well done.

"You look stressed out." a female voice says from behind me. I turn around to see a beautiful blonde angel come over and sit beside me at the bar.

"I am trying to find something, but so far everyone tells me it doesn't exist." I tell her, ignoring her advances. I'm too frustrated to appreciate the flirtation of this very attractive angel.

"Care to share your woes?" she asks me in a suggestive purr.

"I know a faerie who was poisoned by basilisk poison, and she is going to die unless I can find the Garden of Eden." She looks at me perplexed.

"If you wanted me to back off, all you had to do was say so." and she gets up to leave, but hesitates a moment.

"I didn't make up the story." I stare at the countertop. She turns around to look down at me.

"Okay, let's say I believe you, how do you expect to save her if you were to find the Garden of Eden?"

I have absolutely no idea. "A healer told her that the water there will save her from the venom. I think this healer might be a loose cannon if the answers to all my queries are to be believed." I wish someone had told me something that could help. Even if it was just part of a myth rather than based on fact. Anything would have been better than the answers I received.

"I think I may know something about the garden." she says casually.

"Really? Please tell me!" I plead insistently.

"I don't know much so don't start thinking I'm a fountain of knowledge, I don't even know if there is any truth to it." she rushes out. "My father told me a story that his great great grandfather used to tell him." She takes a breath and continues. "It wasn't Eve eating the apple that lead to its destruction. No God can deny indulging in ones desires when they are known for doing the same.

"What happened was greed. It was indeed a place filled with magic and it basically self-destructed. The Gods, Goddesses and angels would harvest its beauty for personal gain. It held the fountain of youth which the Goddesses were coveting to stay beautiful forever. Immortality doesn't always guarantee eternal youthfulness.

"The angels and Gods coveted the fruit and flowers. They found that they gave them great strength and made them even more powerful. Eventually the garden became barren, and the land around it became treacherous. It was just miles and miles of heated land that no one dare cross because they could very well die.

"Because of the greed of so many, the land around the garden became everything everyone wanted to avoid. A place where the worst kinds of being were punished. The ones evicted from heaven would fall, and the ones driven by hate and lust would end up residing." I was so ensnared by her story that it took a minute for the implication to hit me.

"Are you saying...?" I start to say only to be interrupted.

"Yes, the Garden of Eden is in Hell. Or if the story holds true, Hell was created by the garden so no one would ever find it."

"The vilest of creatures both alive and dead are sent there. Why would that be, if the garden was there?" I ask skeptically.

"I didn't say the story was true first of all. Secondly, no one actually knows if the garden actually even existed to begin with. It's a story that has gone from generation to generation for millions of years. Maybe even billions."

"Are there any Gods or angels who could confirm this?" He asks hopefully.

"None that I have ever encountered. Rumour has it that they collectively decided to leave well enough alone since the garden all but disappeared. I think I might have heard that the fruit went rotten and the water went stagnant so it didn't really matter anyway." She says.

"So, even if it does exist the water might not save her anyway?" I really hope that isn't a fact. This is the first lead I have had on its destination and it still isn't all that promising.

"There is someone who might know more about it, but he is a fallen." Damn they are one of the least reliable resources. "His name is Xavier. My father once said his name in accordance to the story. Don't know if he even knows anything, but he might be your best chance."

"Where would I find this Xavier?" I narrow my gaze already anticipating the answer.

"Where do you think silly? In Hell of course." she says teasingly.

"Wow, I'm lucky to have had you sit next to me at the bar." I grin, thankful she decided to try to converse with me.

"It was by no accident." she says before getting up and throwing over her shoulder, "I heard that you were asking about it and I was hoping to have a little fun while I informed you of what I know". She turns and winks at me. "That's an open invitation there handsome." then she walks away.

"Huh, I never even caught her name." I say aloud.

"That was Vivian, one of the eldest angels." the barkeep says.

"Eldest? Why haven't I ever heard of her?" The elders are generally well known since they like to hold there prestige over all the heads of us "younglings".

"Vivian doesn't recognize her own superiority and usually mingles with everyone. A bit of a partier when it comes to an angel, and she enjoys the company of the younger angels." I can tell from the barkeeps expression he may know from experience.

"If she is an elder then her great great grandfather would be what exactly?" I think about where the story came from.

"Long gone by my guess." he says with a shrug.

"I guess I have to find this Xavier." I guess this means I have to go to Hell after all. Maybe I'll be able to find Daemon and Siren while I'm there.

Chapter Eleven

(Maddy)

A real life faerie, who would have thought one would come to Hell. Why anyone would come here by choice is beyond me. I want to leave this place more than anything. Almost anything. I wish that I could be beautiful and find someone to share my very long life with. I may not wish to look as unique as Siren, I do however wish that I had the kind of beauty she has. What I would give to have someone write poetry about my loveliness.

"Siren, what is it like to be a faerie?" I ask her.

"What is it like to be a gorgon?" she counters.

"I imagine very different from your life" I say sadly. It's not really that I am jealous of Siren so much as that I am jealous of any women who isn't a gorgon.

She sighs loudly. "I bet so." She agrees. "I would like to say I don't understand loneliness, but the truth is that I do." That surprises me since she looks like she could get anything she wants. "I know for you it isn't by choice, but because you're afraid of having life like statues. For me I was exiled." She stops walking and slightly turns in my direction. "The truth is, even without my magic, I can see your beauty."

I scoff at that. "That was cruel." I feel a pain deep inside. The feeling that someone beautiful who can never understand your pain, is mocking you.

"I'm serious." she declares more adamantly. "I know you have the power to turn me into stone, but it's not in you to be knowingly malicious. I can tell these things." She smiles at me. "I think you are under a vast misconception that beauty is about how other people see you." She comes over to me and puts her arm around me. One of the snakes on my head lunges at her and she smacks it with a, "Bad snaky." comment and continues on. "Anyone worth having in your life will recognize that beauty is about how you see yourself and is inherently who you are."

"You have no idea how it feels to go your entire life without ever having anyone really see you." I whisper, feeling a tear slide down my cheek.

"Your right, but what I am saying to you is that I see you." She walks up ahead of me silently, telling me this conversation is over. I have no idea if she is right or not, but something inside of me feels better, however miniscule that feeling is.

(SIREN)

As I walk ahead of Maddy, I feel a sharp pain in my chest, I deeply sympathize with the gorgon. I don't know what it's like to never have someone look at me, I do however truly wish I had the power to reverse her curse. I don't even know if it's possible at this point.

Daemon catches up to me and wraps my hand in his. "That was a really sweet things you said to her." he whispers. His face contorts as if he ate something foul before he says, "It goes against my nature to genuinely mean that."

"I really do think her beautiful." I whisper quietly to Daemon, hoping that Maddy can't hear me.

"And I think you are beautiful." he says as he comes to a stop and pulls me back to face him. "I want you so bad Siren." He closes his eyes as if he is in physical pain. He lets me go and softly pushes me away from him.

I shake off the affect his words have on me. When did his words start to matter anyway? I distinctly recall having his opinions matter very little. By very little, I actually mean not at all. I sneak a peek at the man walking next to me, and have to admit that I completely and totally see why he has a different woman every night. He is a very delicious looking man, and if I hadn't been woken up, continuously by his extracurricular hobby, I might have been tempted by him as well.

"See anything you like?" he says with a knowing grin. Dammit he caught me checking him out.

"Yeah" I give him by best sarcastic smile. "I see a smug face I would like to smack." He laughs at that as if he thinks I was joking, little does he know that I was not.

"Is that your kind of foreplay?" Daemon waggles his eyebrows at me. "Because I think I could totally be game for that."

I shake my head. "You are never going to give up are you?"

"I will give up after I have your luscious body." He states with a laugh.

"So I guess you will never give up." I wink.

"You guys are incorrigible." Maddy mutters from behind us. That makes Daemon's smile widen. The cocky bastard.

Out of the darkness I hear a maniacal laugh. "Daemon, Daemon, Daemon! To what do we owe the pleasure?" Out of the shadows comes a tall, very good looking man with blonde hair and blue eyes. Though he has a face of innocents, something about his tone is contradictory.

"Shit." Daemon says under his breath. Louder he says "Gunnar, the pleasure is all mine".

"I'm sure it is." Gunnar eyes me up and licks his lips. "Looks like you have a delicious treat there Daemon. Mind sharing?" He walks over to me but Daemon blocks his path. "Come on man, it wouldn't be the first time we shared a woman." The way he is looking at me almost makes me feel like a piece of meat. I'm just not sure if it's figuratively or literally.

"This one is all mine." Daemon says with authority.

"Oh. A challenge! How delightful." Gunnar mocks as he approaches us. Something behind us grabs his attention and he bursts out in riotous laughter. "Since when have you started keeping the company of gorgons?"

I hear a gasp of outrage from behind me, but I am unable to turn around and see if she's alright. "That would be my bad." I give a small wave from behind Daemon.

"A woman with attitude, I like." Gunnar smirks. Before I can even register what is happening there is a blur running toward us. Daemon adjusts his stance and throws a punch at seemingly nothing. Gunnar stumbles backwards before throwing a punch of his own.

"Go home Gunnar." Daemon growls out.

"Not without her." he points to me with a sadistic smile showing a pair of canines. Is he a vampire?

"You are not going to have her." Daemon rushes at Gunnar and fists are flying. They both look like they are receiving as many hits as they are throwing.

Gunnar looks at me and I notice the opening he has created. Daemon is no longer an obstacle that Gunnar needs to worry about. With more speed then I have ever seen before, Gunnar grabs me from behind and is holding me against his chest with his one hand cupping my chin and the other wrapped around my waist.

He whispers in my ear "I wonder if you're as tasty as you look?"

"Maybe you should take a bite and find out." I say seductively. Daemon growls at my words and I see hurt behind his eyes. I smile and wink at him and his expression morphs to one of confusion.

I feel him turn my neck so he has better access to my throat as he licks a line up towards my ear. A flash of pain is all I feel before he is throwing me away from him trying to spit out my blood. The now confirmed vampire is holding his throat while making choking sounds.

"You should never take candy from a stranger." I say in my most maternal tone. I can't help but laugh as he continues to cough.

"It burns." he chokes out. "What have you done to me?"

"I believe sir, you bit me." I say in my fakest British accent.

"You tricked me." he accosts me.

"I did nothing of the sort. You were going to drink from me anyway, I just told you that you were allowed to. There's a difference. Take responsibility for your own actions."

"I can't believe there is a kind of blood a vampire can't drink" Maddy says from the behind me. I look over and she is getting up off the ground where she was hidden behind a rock. Huh, she must have gone there when Gunnar attacked me.

"What is wrong with your blood?" Gunnar asks me.

"Let's just say I could be used as a biological weapon" I chuckle. "As in its biological." I laugh a bit harder while Daemon and Maddy both cock their heads at me.

"What are you? And don't try and tell me you're a comedian, because I won't believe it." Gunnar sounds more curious then angry.

"If I tell you, I'll have to kill you." I smile at him and he takes a step back. Who knew I could unnerve a vampire? Who knew I would ever meet one? We only have incubi and succubi which is similar in nature I suppose. They all require close contact.

"I'll be on my way." With that Gunner walks past us, giving me a wide birth. How rude.

Daemon comes over and takes me into his arms. They feel so good wrapped around me and I know I shouldn't, but I hug him back. "That scared me for a minute there." he whispers into my ear.

"I knew my blood would burn him." I hesitate before adding, "Well I was really hoping so. Without my magic it could have gone either way." He holds me tighter and then as if he finally realized what he was doing, he pulls back and steps away from me while clearing his throat.

"Shall we go?" He gestures for us to go ahead.

"That was wild." Maddy sounds giddy. "I seriously have never seen that happen before." Her tone sounds like it has a smile in it.

As we walk for a few minutes, I see Daemon constantly looking at my neck. "What are you looking at?"

"You wound isn't healing." he points out. I touch my neck and look at my bloodstained finger.

"Shit!" The poison is slowing down my healing. "I'm sure it will start to heal soon." I lie.

"Siren!" He stills me with a hand on my arm. He moves closer to take a better look at the wound. "Does it feel like it's healing at all?"

"I don't know." I say honestly. "Maybe it's just healing a lot slower." Oh, how I hope that's the truth.

We continue walking when my bite becomes itchy. I scratch it only to remove a scab and reopen it. "It looks like it's healing at least." Daemon nods toward my neck.

"Is that what's happening?" I have never experienced this brand of torture. It's so itchy, but when I scratch it, it feels like I'm peeling off my own flesh. I go to scratch the itchiness again and this time my flesh feels much smoother. "How does it look?"

"It looks like a scar now." Daemon sounds relieved. "I think it will heal completely."

"How are you feeling?" Maddy stands beside me while looking straight ahead. I found out it's because it ensures that if I look over at her, we won't make eye contact.

I take a shaky breath. "Scared." I try to hide it, but when a wound that isn't even mortally damaging takes minutes to heal, that's a detrimental sign. What if something that would fatally wound a mortal happens to me? I am little more than mortal myself.

"I'm sorry that Xavier's isn't closer." she says in a low voice.

"We'll make it there if it's the last thing I do." It very well might be.

"Let's hope that isn't the case." Daemon puts his arm around me. He seems to be touchy feely today. I wonder what that's about.

ABOUT AN HOUR LATER we turn left into another section of this cave. It's extremely bright in this part. As I look around I notice the sconces on the wall. I don't mean candles either, nope. I mean huge flaming torches. As we walk through them, I realize there are also doors going into the rock. These are homes.

"The rock is habitable?" I ask in disbelief, pointing to the doors.

Daemon and Maddy both laugh, but its Maddy who answers. "A fair majority of Hell's population is living in these rocks."

"Where do the rest of them live?"

Maddy and Daemon look at each other and this time Daemon just points up. "It's cooler down here which is really saying something about above ground."

"Wait, there is more up there?"

"Oh yeah. Too bad most of the things that live up there are from your worst nightmares." Daemon answers again.

"And I thought down here was bad."

"We're almost there." Maddy announces. "It's only a few doors down."

WE KNOCK ON THE STONE door and a petite woman with long golden hair and horns answers the door. Other than the little horns she looks like a human.

"Maddy." The woman greet her with hug without looking her into her eyes.

"We need to see Xavier if he's free." Maddy tells the demoness.

"Uh, yeah he is. He's always free to see you Maddy. You should know that by now." Maddy blushes a little.

"This way." The servant says as we follow behind through an open room with doors around it. She leads us to one of those doors. "Xavier, Maddy's here to see you."

"Let her in." comes a male voice from inside the room. It's fairly deep, but also smooth.

We walk into the room and Xavier, who has curly, dark brown shoulder length hair and a goatee, looks up and appears a little taken aback by Daemon and I who are also in the room. "How may I help you?" the fallen angel quirks an eyebrow, looking to the side of Maddy before taking in the rest of us.

"My friends here need to find the Garden of Eden and I thought maybe you would know something about it?" At the mention of the garden, the man noticeably flinches.

"I'm sorry, I can't help you." he tells us.

"Have you ever heard of the garden's existence?" I ask him, needing desperately for him to say yes.

"Not only have I heard of it, I have been there. No good will come from it." He informs me and then glances toward Maddy. "And I hope you don't plan on going there."

She looks at the ground as she says, "I was thinking that maybe it could cure my curse."

I see a look cross Xavier face, but it's gone before I could decipher it. Also interesting. "That place is more likely to be a detriment then a cure. What do you think made me fall?"

"The garden is why you aren't in Heaven anymore?" Daemon asks.

"It's also where the seven deadly sins came from. Gluttony, eating the magic fruit that created more strength and power. Vanity, using the fountain of youth. Lust, well when you are stronger and younger, it comes with the territory, along with pride. Greed, because we all wanted more and more. It was never enough. Envy, well I think you can figure that one out, and with the kind of envy that comes from that kind of power, well then came wrath. Sloth, well no one was productive anymore because they were addicted to the garden. Many of us fell, and we now govern parts of hell. I govern this part." I have no idea what to say to that.

"I just need the river to heal, to rid the poison from my body." He looks me up and down and Daemon makes a fierce sound from next to me. Xavier smiles at him and holds his hands up in surrender.

"I'm sorry. I can't in good consciousness tell you where it is. I don't think it matters even if I did. From what I know of it, it's dead anyway." He looks at Maddy. "It will not help you." With that he dismisses us.

As we walk out of Xavier's place Maddy says, "I have never seen him like that before. I'm really sorry, I thought he would help us."

Chapter Twelve

(Ezekiel)

After searching for hours for the address (or at least Hells equivalent) to Xavier's, I finally find it. It's in an area with many homes built into the brimstone of hell. I knock on the door and a little demoness answers.

"Can I speak to Xavier?" I say, more of a statement then a question really.

"He is quite popular today." she says as she leads me through an open space area and to his 'meetings' room. There are a couple of comfy chairs on either side of a fire place. "He will meet you here in a few minutes." She closes the door,

"Thank you."

Not long after, I hear footsteps descending and the door opens. In comes a tall man with dark brown shoulder length curly hair and a goatee. His eyes are dark blue with a gold ring. "To what do I owe the pleasure of having a divine angel in my home?" He says 'divine' with distaste.

"I am looking for the Garden of Eden and was told you would be able to help me."

"Ah, you must know the faerie and demon that were here earlier." He suggest with a nod.

"They were here? You know of faeries?" I have never met anyone who really knew of them by sight like that.

"Yes to both. I didn't know at first, but once I took an inspection and noticed her pallor it all made sense. Her lover seemed to have taken offence to my scrutiny." He chuckles at the memory.

"Lover?" I ask bewildered.

"Oh yes, that Daemon." He clarifies.

"They are not lovers." I argue.

"Well he certainly reacted like one if I do say so myself."

I shake the thought away. "Did you tell them where the garden was?"

"I couldn't do it. I'm sorry but I can't tell you either." He does sound apologetic, but that seems insignificant.

"I know it's in Hell." My tone is harsh, demanding answers.

"It could be yes. If you want to find it, you will have to find it on your own. If you run into the other three, make sure Maddy doesn't go into the garden." He uses his own tone of authority.

"Maddy?" I ask perplexed.

"The little gorgon girl with the other two." I see affection on his face as his eyes soften. "Just, if you run into them, protect her. It's all I ask."

"You want me to protect this filthy gorgon and you can't tell me where the garden is?" I'm a little peeved at his request since I was the one who came for answers.

"Do not talk about her like that!" he growls. He sits back in his chair, taking a breath. "I am not telling you for your own protection. There is nothing to accomplish there, but pain and suffering."

"I can't promise to protect her." I say matter-of-factly. "I refuse to make promises I'm not sure I can keep."

"Understood. Now, you can find your own way out, I'm sure." Just like that I am dismissed.

I walk out looking around to see if there is any sign to which direction they may have gone. I see a demon man hanging around outside his little rock home.

"Excuse me? Have you seen a navy haired woman with a blonde man and a gorgon? I ask him impatiently.

"Oh yes, I have." He looks to his right and nods down the tunnel. "Went that way."

"Thank you." I walk in the same direction, hopeful I am not too far behind them.

"OH ANGEL," I HEAR IN a hissing sound. "Have you come here to play?" The voice does not sound like something I want to waste my time encountering. Unfortunately it would appear I don't have much of a choice. Up ahead I see a hell bound creature that has a human profile, but his body and face is scaly like a snake. He is wearing worn out clothes covering most of him and his eyes are yellow. His forked tongue exits his mouth as he hisses at me, and he has very short spiky hair on his head.

"I would really like to make it by you without incident." I try to calmly warn the creature.

He cackles and the sound pierces my ears with its high frequency. "I don't think so angel." Before I can react he is throwing a boomerang like object at me and it goes into my shoulder, when I pull it out I see that it is a bone carved into a knife. The demon is running at me with two daggers, one in each hand and they too look like they are made of bones.

He swipes one at me but I block it with the dagger from my shoulder. I swipe out and catch his arm and back away just before he nicks my throat. Too close. I pull out my sword of white light and thrust it in his direction. He parries it with his two daggers and kicks his foot out into my stomach.

I stumble backwards but catch my balance just as he is running at me. I step to the side and he passes me while fumbling over his feet. He turns around with his daggers still in hand, but I strike first. As my sword hits him, white light bursts from him, almost like a small explosion and then there is nothing left of him.

I hope Siren and Daemon didn't gain much more ground on me, I am the only one who might be able to help them find the garden. I bet they don't even know it's in Hell. Why would they? No one would look here for a garden that is biblically known for its perfection and beauty. I hope I can find them before they leave hell.

(GWENDOLYN)

I come back to hell and what do I hear talk of? Daemon and his freak lover. I clench my fists at the thought of how Daemon seems so protective of this Siren. I have to save him from her clutches before she takes complete control of him. He has always been mine and I am not going to let her have him now. Not her or anyone else.

"Hello Gwendolyn." I turn around and there is Gunnar. "When did you get back?"

"A couple of days ago" I answer

"You are never going to guess who I ran into today." he says with enthusiasm.

"Daemon?" I ask dryly.

"Uh, yeah." He agrees nonplussed. "He was with..."

"A weird looking woman." I finish for him.

"Yes." Now he sounds suspicious. "And a gorgon."

"A gorgon? Why would he share the company of one of those filthy creatures?"

"Looked like it was his woman's idea." He answers.

"Of course it was." I shake my head. "We need to save him from those two vile women." My wheels start turning. "Want to help?"

He gives a devilish smile. "I don't think I want to get involved in this one Gwenny. That freaky chick with him, is something from another world. I am not getting tangled with that thing." He sounds so adamant.

"What did she do?"

"Her blood was like acid going down." He makes a face at the memory.

"This time I am going to make sure she is gone for good." My fists clench again.

"This time?" He asks me with a questioning smile.

"I helped her ex-fiancé get her back. Looks like she got away." I start pacing around the cave area. It isn't extravagant, but we demons don't need much. Just souls.

"What are you going to do now?"

I have the perfect plan in mind, and there is no way I am going to tell anyone until it's been executed

Chapter Thirteen

(Daemon)

"Are you alright to keep going?" I look at Siren and note that she is paler then before, even the blue in her eyes have become duller. I can't stand the fact that the poison is enveloping more and more of her and there is absolutely nothing I can do to make her better.

"I can do it." She gives me a weak smile that doesn't light any part of her beautiful face. As unconvincing as it is, I want to keep moving if at all possible. Even though we don't know where we are going, I still want to get there as soon as we can. Losing Siren isn't an option. I don't know if I will ever have her, but knowing that somewhere out there she exists, would still pacify me. But if she dies, I have no idea what I will do, and that scares the ever living hell (mind my pun) out of me.

"Siren, I know it's important to find the garden, but we don't know where we are even going. We could be walking further and further away from it. If you need to stop for a second, it's okay." Maddy says to her. I have to say that I am more than one hundred percent in agreement with her.

Siren sighs. I know for her that this is literally life and death. "I don't know what to do right now." For the first time since I have met her, I see a crack in her façade. "I want to keep going." She sounds so doubtful it almost breaks me. "But where am I going really? I have not a clue. We could walk until my last breath and not find anything. Where is the garden? Is it in heaven? I think that would make the most sense because of how it's known biblically and yet, here we are, in Hell." The defeat I see in her is like a gut punch. If she gives up now, then what hope do we really have?

"We are going to find it" I wrap my arm around her shoulder and pull her toward me. "We have to." I don't mention that I can't imagine what the world would be like without her. How can I admit that to her when I don't know what it means to myself? I know I want her. I have since the moment I first saw her. I know that she is the first woman who hasn't fallen wantonly into my arms begging for more. It's frustrating that I want her so badly that it takes all my energy not to kiss her, to demand more from her. If I try anything she will likely pull away and then what chance do I have?

"I know we are going to try, but what if we fail?" she whispers to me.

"That is not an option" I state sternly. "So long as you have breath, I will try everything in my power to preserve it." And I will.

She stops suddenly and turns to me with those big, gorgeous blue eyes and I see tears in them. "Thank you Daemon." She walks over to me and wraps her arms around my torso. Stunned for a second I just stand there like an idiot before sense kicks in and I take advantage of being able to hug her back. She holds on to me tighter as if I am some saving grace. I kiss the top of her head and revel in the smell of her.

A throat clearing comes from behind us. "Are you two going to keep moving or should I give you some space?" Maddy interrupts our moment.

I look to the side of her and say, "You don't have to join us you know."

Even out of the corner of my eye, I notice her flinch at my words and I feel like a complete asshole. Siren narrows her eyes at me and pinches me in the side, confirming she does too.

"I know, but I'm hoping something will cure me." I see her head go up in a stubborn and defiant stance. "I just want to be beautiful."

"I'm sorry if I offended you." The strange thing is that I truly am. I haven't felt guilt since the first couple of years of my killing. I wonder if that one little tear I touched is to blame for this. The funny thing is, I don't regret it. I did at first, but I am starting to feel like the old me again. The real me. At my apology, Siren gives me a small smile.

"You are more than welcome to come with us." Siren says to the girl.

"I really need to do this. No one can really understands how it feels to have to watch where you look, because in a heartbeat you could kill someone." She gives a self-deprecating laugh. "I guess we know where that saying 'if looks could kill' comes from."

"I don't know if we will figure something out that can help you." Siren gently takes Maddy's hand. The snakes seem to have given up on attacking, not that it stopped Siren from approaching. "I do know that regardless of anything, I will be here to help you try."

"Do you think it's that impossible?" Maddy sounds heartbreakingly defeated.

"I don't know if anything is impossible, but when it comes to curses, there are a lot of things that are improbable. Remember, just because it seems unlikely doesn't mean it is." Siren gives a little smile looking straight ahead of her. "Just like it's improbable that I am going to survive the poison." Her words are like a knife to the chest. "That doesn't mean it's impossible." I feel a little relief knowing she hasn't given up, but the reminder is there that she could die. As if I have had a second to forget it, but I hate hearing the words, especially from her.

"I hope we can save you" Maddy says quietly. "I know in comparison, my problem is so small." She sounds ashamed of herself.

"No, it is different. I haven't gone my whole life feeling like a pariah. I may die, but we all will someday, even if it takes millions of years for it to happen." She gives me a look, maybe reminding me that I too have an expiration date. "I just might have it happen sooner."

I'm so intrigued by her strength and the way she is. I know firsthand that she is a deadly weapon. She isn't afraid of torturing someone, and I believe she might even enjoy it on some sadistic level. It's her compassion that has me flabbergasted. Here she is, dying, and yet she still tries to remain strong for a girl who feels guilty for her vanity. Siren genuinely wants Maddy to be happy, is trying to see things through the girls eyes. For some reason it makes me want to kiss her, which is weird for me because at one point, I am pretty sure I would have gone into anaphylactic shock from the empathy.

I have no idea what is happening to me, and to be totally honest, I don't think I completely dislike it either. I'm a little scared of what this means. Siren looks over at me and notices me staring at her and I quickly look away, even though I know I was caught. I can't help it though, I enjoy looking at her. I think about Maddy, and suddenly I understand how she feels. No one has ever been able to look at her the way I am looking at Siren, the way many, many, many women have looked at me. I feel a little empathy myself. I take a swallow and feel a lump in my throat. Is it swelling? Oh no, it's not, it's just an emotion. Shit, that's even worse.

"What is that?" Siren asks as she turns her head, as if trying to listen to something and hear better.

"What are you talking about?" I listen and I hear the faint sounds of music playing.

"Do you hear that music?" she asks me.

"Yeah." I answer as Maddy slowly nods.

"Sounds like a party." Maddy points out. "I don't know what they would be celebrating though. With demons it could be anything, they really enjoy an excuse to let loose and indulge in any sin they can."

"Should we turn around?" Siren seems a little nervous.

"I think it should be okay to go through. They're too busy having a good time." I point out. Demons like to take a break from the everyday grind too, just like everyone else. There is a good chance they won't even notice us, but if they do, it's highly unlikely they will mind our presence. They will however likely have a search party for us in the morning. They love their hunting too, and a prey that comes willingly isn't a fun kill. I probably shouldn't tell Siren that last part. "I have never seen you afraid of anything."

"It's easy not to be scared of much when my powers are greater than most. Now that I don't have them and I'm weakening by the moment, fear becomes a real thing." Siren says conversationally. I can barely even tell that she is afraid by the way her voice remains even.

"Are you ready to go to a demonic party?" I ask the two of them. They both nod but they seem unsure about the question.

AS WE GET CLOSER TO where the party is being held I see more and more demons heading toward it. The music is haunting in its beauty as it borders on creepy and majestic. It appears to be a black tie affair. Looking around and I see demons of all kinds dressed up and dancing. I know we are a little underdressed, but there is nothing to be done about it since we don't have a change of clothes. The party is in the cave right where we have to go through to get to the other side. Even though this part of the cave is wide open, there are demons in every section.

We begin our way when someone pulls Siren away from me. I look to see who it is, and it's a demon with huge horns and somewhat hairy face. He is looking at her like he want to do more than dance with her. Maddy looks around as if she is hoping someone will sweep her off her feet, but everyone gives her a wide birth. I offer Maddy my hand and we make our way onto the floor without ever taking my eyes off of Siren.

"Thank you for the dance Daemon." Maddy whispers to me.

"I figured you wanted a dance partner." I keep watching the man dancing with Siren when he says something in her ear and she lightly laughs. Is she flirting with him? My grip on Maddy gets tighter as I watch them dancing.

"Ouch!" Maddy hisses. She sees where I am looking and turns around to check out why I'm so irritated. "Ah ha, it all makes sense now." She shakes her head and I hear a bit of a smile in her voice. "You're afraid that guy is going to steal your girl away."

"I just don't like the way he's looking at her." I correct defensively.

"Yeah, okay." She sounds sarcastic as she says it.

I see the demon's hands slip lower and lower as he is whispering in her ear. I snarl at the sight and rush over to them and push him away. I grab Siren and slam my lips onto hers kissing her harshly. I want to show all these men who she belongs too. When I feel her respond I slip my tongue into her mouth and hear her moan. Just as I pull her closer to me I feel her stiffen and pull back.

"Thanks for the rescue, but I think I can take it from here." She says as if she is shaking off the moment.

"Care to dance?" I can't help but ask, right now any excuse to have her close seems like a good one. She looks like she is just about to agree when a voice cuts in. The voice is right beside me, and way to close to my ear.

"Daemon, you're back." The woman sounds hungry. She runs her hand up my arm and wedges herself between Siren and me. "You look just as good as the last time you were here. Remember how we went all night long?" I know she deliberately said it so Siren would back off.

"Miss, you seem to be falling out of your dress." Siren feigns boredom. This woman gives Siren a nasty look, but turns back to me.

"Baby, wouldn't you like to go for another round? I could occupy your time for hours."

I clear my throat before speaking, "I'm sorry, but I'm here with someone else." I try to gently push this ravenous demoness away from me, but she pulls herself closer to me rubbing herself against my crotch. This time I push her away forcefully enough that she stumbles backwards before catching her balance.

"I said I wasn't interested now move out of my way." I growl at her. I grab Siren and pull her against me for a dance, effectively turning away from what's her name. I seriously can't remember, and don't really remember our night together. As if she was the only one I went all night with. Nope. A few weeks ago I would have been raring to go with her. Not so much now. Actually not at all.

"I'm sorry about that." I whisper into Siren's ear and pull her tightly against me.

"It's funny how some women have selective eye sight and suddenly can't see another woman standing right next to the man she wants to pursue." She shakes her head in a "how sad" kind of way.

(SIREN)

Some women think they are so entitled that they will go for another woman's man. I know Daemon isn't mine, but she didn't know that. She just made an effort to push me out so she could have him all to herself. For some reason that bothered me. I mean after that searing kiss he gave me, if he had left with her, I think I would have kicked him in the junk. The most surprising part is that he blew her off and chose me, even though he could have had a sure thing.

"You're the woman I want." he murmurs, his lips so close to my ear I can feel them brush against it.

"Daemon." I whisper breathlessly, and I feel him smile as he lightly nips my earlobe. I wrap my arms around his neck, holding his head tighter toward me when I feel him kissing my neck. I tilt my head, giving him better access when he pulls me even tighter. So tight I feel how hard he is and he moans.

"I want to take you in a dark corner Siren." His kisses turn into sucking and nipping. "Oh Siren," he says before taking my lips in a kiss that says possession. His tongue possesses my mouth with hard thrusts. He lifts his head and both of us are breathing heavily. I look up at him and remember where we are and what we're doing and most importantly, who I am doing them with. I abruptly push him away from me. Something passes across Daemon's face before he composes himself.

"I..." I don't even know what to say, so I say nothing as I look around for Maddy, and spot her leaning against the rock wall, staring at the ground with her shoulders hunched. I make my way over to her.

"Looked like you and Daemon were getting cozy out there." she mumbles when I approach her.

"Oh yeah, that." I feel the blush on my cheeks. "That was nothing."

She laughs lightly. "Who are you trying to kid?"

I don't know what to say to that. I honestly don't even know what it is I am feeling for that demon, other than it isn't the distain I remember feeling when I first met him. "Why are you standing over here all by yourself?"

She laughs without humour. "Why do you think?"

"I'm sorry." I say quietly to her, feeling ashamed that I didn't have the foresight not to ask a question about the obvious. How stupid.

"I'm used to it." Her voice has a dejection to it that speaks loudly, only what it says is 'no matter how often you're rejected, you never really get used to it'.

I look back on the dancefloor and see women flocking Daemon. He has a smile on his face that says how much he loves it, but it dims when we make eye contact. I turn away from the spectacle.

"That is the kind of man Daemon is. A man who loves the ladies, all of them." I nod toward him so Maddy can see what I am talking about.

"He doesn't look at them like he looks at you." Maddy answers in acknowledgement.

"That's only because I'm a challenge he has yet to win."

One of the women puts her hands on his chest and whispers in his ear. He smiles at her and some kind of adrenaline rushes through me. What is wrong with me? It must be the poison messing with my mind. Yes, that has to be it. It's amped up when I see Daemon whisper something back to the blonde bimbo and she giggles.

"For someone who doesn't care you're fists are clenched awfully tight, and if lasers could come from your eyes, I'm pretty sure a couple demonic women would be disintegrated."

"I don't care what he does." I deny far too quickly. Maddy just raises an eyebrow in accusation.

The way he is looking at her speaks of all things carnal. I need to get out of here before I'm sick. Why do I feel sick? As I push away from the rock wall to go somewhere quieter, Daemon looks over and winks at me. What. The...?

The blonde one takes Daemons hand and starts dancing in a way that should be illegal, but it's Hell so everything goes. He dances with her, and I have to leave fast. I walk past a bunch of demons, making my way through the crowd, when I finally get to a quiet section where very few creatures are.

I still have no idea why the scene back there even bothers me. I must be more compromised from the poison then I thought. Maybe it's because I saw this side of Daemon and thought that maybe it meant something it didn't. I don't know. I am not standing there very long when I feel someone come up to me and a voice whispers in my ear. "Something bothering you?" I abruptly turn around at the voice and come face to face with Daemon.

I look into his face for a moment, so close to mine. "No, I just needed a second away from the crowd." I lie.

"Sure you did." He takes a step back. "Should we get Maddy and continue?"

"Don't you want some alone time with those bimbos?" I snap at him.

"Nah, they were to forward for my liking." he shrugs nonchalantly.

I laugh at that which is completely void of humour. "Yeah, I'm sure you hate women who grope you in public."

He smiles, the kind full of mischief which makes my knees weak. Damn this poison. He leans in to me and whispers, "I was only wishing it was you instead." His words take me aback, I gasp loud enough that he hears, and his smile widens.

"I..." Maddy comes around the corner, saving me from some sentence that I couldn't even finish. Would I have said 'I wish it was too?' I really don't know. Instead I turn to Maddy and say, "Ready to keep going?" Daemon's smile fades before he turns around to acknowledge her as well.

"Yes please. These social gatherings just remind me of my inadequacies."

"Okay, let's keep going." Daemon says on a sigh, before turning back to me with a look that almost looks crestfallen. I don't understand demons.

(DAEMON)

I suspect that I might have been close to breaking through Siren's barriers. I was paying attention to her while I was talking to that hottie. The blonde was hot, but she didn't hold a candle to the dark haired faerie I want so desperately. That faerie was about to say something, and I feel it could have been a game changer, but then Maddy interrupted us. When I was peeking up at Siren, she looked like she wanted to cut down the demon women around me. I thought I saw blood lust in her gaze and thought that maybe I finally won and broke through that wall. Looks like I might have to try harder.

Chapter Fourteen

(Ezekiel)

I walk for hours when I hear the faint sounds of music. As I get closer and closer I see all different types of Hell's creatures dancing in their gowns and suits. Its surreal seeing them all dressed up looking as if they don't have any interest in sucking the life out of mortals.

As I make my way through the party, I see many of them turn to look at me. The males looking as if they want to gut me and the women with a lusty twinkle in their eyes. One of these said women saunter over and place her hands on my chest while slowly caressing.

"Would you care to dance handsome angel?" The disgust in me is too hard to tamp down as I push her away.

"Get off of me you parasite." Her face drops and she appears to be surprisingly hurts. Oh well. No need to worry about the feelings of anything from this God forsaken place. Literally God forsaken!

I push my way through the crowd, now hearing calls from demons. One of them jumps in front of me while holding up a sword that looks like it's forged out of the fires of Hell. I slowly take a step back, trying to hide the twinge of fear I am most definitely feeling.

"I just want to get through." I say to the huge brute of a demon.

He gives me a menacing smile where I can see his yellowed teeth that look sharp enough to be used as weapons on their own. "I don't think so." he swipes the sword at head level. I manage to duck in the nick of time, but I wasn't quite fast enough as I realize the smell of burnt hair permeating the air.

I don't have much time to react so I swipe out my foot and take his legs out from under him, making him land on his back. Hard. I stand over him and I am about to grab for my sword when he swipes his foot out, taking my legs out from under me. I guess I should have seen that one coming right? He's quick as he strikes with his sword, going for my head again.

I roll out of the way as I feel the heat of the weapon far too close to my neck for comfort. I try to get back up and make it to my hands and knees when I feel a searing pain catch me in the side. My hands and knees slip as I fall onto my stomach. I cannot die here after living for so long. I will not die in Hell.

I have my sword materialize in my hand and roll onto my back. I manage to block the next blow of the sword. In my peripheral vision, I can see the crowd has congregate around us, but thankfully none of them look like they want to join the fray. When our swords collide together, there is smoke coming from the area where they are joined. I can feel the heat of the fire running up into my handle and burning my hands. In turn it looks like he is experiencing some kind of discomfort as well, but it doesn't look anything like what I feel.

I thrust my foot up, catching him in the stomach and pushing him away. As I catch my balance, I take a step forward and swipe my sword out. Luckily I did catch his head. As it falls off, he bursts into a flash of light before his head even hits the ground. As I turn around expecting a fight, I see all the other creatures take a step back.

"Does anyone else have a problem with my passing through?" I ask with more confidence then I really feel.

I see them shake their heads as they part, making room for me to get through the crowd. As I make my way through, I ask a few of the creatures if they have seen a dark blue haired beauty, to which many of them point in the direction that they saw them vacate to. I thank them with a smile and follow in the direction that they pointed to.

As I walk down the cave, I see no sign of Siren and Daemon. I know they are probably too far ahead for me to catch up to any time soon, but I hope they stop to rest, giving me time to catch up. I know they have no idea I am on their trail or that they are closer to the garden then they know. Do they even have a destination that they are aiming for? Are they walking mindlessly and blindly? To this I wish I had an answer.

(SIREN)

We walk and we walk through the dark tunnels that are only lit by torches lined sporadically along the wall. My legs are starting to feel achy from all the travelling with very little rest. Well, that and the poison I'm sure.

Here I am pushing myself, having the poison spread through my body with every heartbeat and in the end, we don't even know if we are going in the right direction. We have no idea where this garden is, and here I am literally killing myself to find something that might not even exist. I sigh loudly.

"Everything okay?" Daemon asks as he takes my hand in his and gives me a concerned look.

"Yeah." I lie.

"What's on your mind?" He stops me and looks into my eyes as if trying to find the answer there. I look away.

"I... I just need to rest a moment." It's the truth.

"That's a good idea." he leans against the wall and pulls me towards his chest. I don't fight it, I don't have the energy to do so. Then he whispers in my ear, "There's something else bothering you."

I don't want to sound like a weak little girl by telling him my fears. I'm not ready for him to see that side of me, to feel exposed. I laugh to myself. He already has seen me without my magic as I slowly die. What's a little fear? "I just don't know if we are even walking in the right direction. We could be wasting time going the wrong way." I look down at the ground. "I just don't want to die."

At my admission I feel his arms tighten around me. "We are going to find this garden."

"What if we don't?" I whisper, realizing for the first time that we are alone. That Maddy has given us privacy by strolling a little ways behind us and has stopped far enough away that she can't hear our conversation.

"That's not even an option." he growls adamantly.

"You're right, it's a real possibility. Actually, it's the most likely outcome." I feel a stray tear for the first time. He wipes it away with his thumb.

"Stop talking like that." I pull away from him and lean on the wall beside him, sliding down it to sit. He sits down beside me and rests his hand on my leg. "We are going to get through this."

"We?" I look over at him. "I am probably going to die and you will move on to greener pastures." And forget all about me.

"Never!" He gives my leg a squeeze. "You are not going to die and if you do..." he gulps but doesn't finish his sentence. I look over at him, but he just looks at the wall on the other side of the tunnel. I don't know what he was going to say, but it looks as though he isn't about to continue.

"When you touched my tear, did you feel any of its magic?" I can't help but ask him.

He looks at his hand as he slowly shakes his head. "No, but I have touched your tears before and I have already been changed. That might be why."

I just sit there, mouth agape. "What? When?"

He turns his head to me so quickly I swear he has to have whiplash. "What? Nothing!" The look of horror on his face is suddenly washed away and replaced with his usual smug one.

"What are you talking about Daemon?" I ask more slowly, just in case he suddenly became dim.

"Nothing!" He sighs. "What I said was I couldn't feel the magic."

"Yes, you said that." I continue. "Because you touched my tear before?"

"Siren, let's not talk about this anymore." He puts his arm around me and pulls me to his chest.

"How?" I demand. He doesn't say anything, and I can tell I'm not going to get any answers from him. Instead he calls to Maddy.

"You can sit over here with us." I peer up at him and glare, but he ignores it. I try to pull out from under his arm, but he wraps his other one around me to stop my escape. Smooth.

I feel his breath against my ear as he whispers "You aren't going anywhere yet."

Maddy sits down beside Daemon, but doesn't say anything. It's easy to forget she's even here most of the time. I wonder what has made her come along.

"Why are you coming with us?" She flinches as if I slapped her. "What I mean is, what makes you want to come?"

"Oh!" she says relieved. "I think I have made my reasons clear."

"Yeah, but we could be going the wrong way. You could have better odds without us."

She laughs without humour. "Maybe you are. As of now, you're the only hope I have." I nod in understanding. "Besides, my problem pales in comparison to yours."

"Stop!" Daemon growls. "We are going to save Siren."

His vehemence makes me look at him and his face is dark. When he looks down at me, I can see the demon inside of him, but as he studies my face I see it slowly fade away.

"I'm sorry to upset you." Maddy apologizes with sincerity. "I know you care about her and don't want anything to happen. You're nothing like the rumours I have heard about the big bad Daemon."

Daemon turns in Maddy's direction with an odd expresson on his face. Not so much as if he's offended as much as curious about her words. He looks back at me and takes a step back. "I do, don't I?" he whispers to himself. "I mean, I knew I cared, but I didn't realize the implications of it until now."

"What are you talking about?" I ask with absolutely no finesse.

"I thought I just wanted a piece of ass." he shoots back at me.

"I naturally assumed you must care a little if you were willing to rescue me from the faerie king." a small laugh escapes at his expense.

"Yeah, well, I was assuming it was because it wouldn't be much fun banging a dead chick." I can't help but shake my head at that.

"Of course everything is about sex with you isn't it?"

"Apparently not." He sounds offended by his own emotions, which makes me laugh out loud. "What's so funny?" his tone is filled with accusations.

"You! You're funny."

Maddy is just looking at us like we are crazy before adding "Seriously?" with an eye roll and a shake of her head. Poor girl doesn't realize she is with a couple of lunatics. One of those lunatics also being a pervert and the other being well.... Me.

"When and how did this happen?" he sounds almost a little dazed. "One minute I am being entranced by a beautiful blonde, and the next I am running around hell with a navy haired faery. You did this to me didn't you?" He does not sounds like he is joking, but rather like he thinks I wanted this.

I laugh. Much harder then I should have I'm sure, but I couldn't help it. I hunch over laughing. "Are... you... serious?" I say between bouts of laughter. "I couldn't stand you." His face doesn't look amused at all, but I see a flicker of pain before its masked. Something inside of me feels guilty for putting that look on his face and my laughter slowly subsides... very, very slowly. What? That was funny.

"Seriously though, I did not use my magic on you. This situation is all you."

"Well, you didn't have to laugh that hard at the idea." He narrows his eyes at me.

"Sorry." Weirdly I don't sound all that sorry at all. "It's just that, if I was going to put a spell on you before all this, it would have been to take away your erections." His jaw drops open at my admission. "Well it's true." I shrug.

"Wow, you're cruel."

I hear some laughter and look over to see Maddy laughing at us. "You two are made for each other."

Daemon and I look at each other and then look away very quickly, maybe too quickly and Maddy catches it. "You are so blind." She says with disbelief. I have no idea what to say so I just stay quiet. A quick look at Daemon tells me he feels the exact same way.

Chapter Fifteen

(Daemon)

We have been walking for hours and I am still replaying Maddy's words in my head over and over again. I do care about Siren, more than I have cared about anyone for as long as I can remember. My father made sure of that one. I cannot go back to the weak demon with a conscience and sympathy. She must be using magic on me to make me feel this way, it's the only logical explanation. Someone who hasn't felt anything but loathing, can't suddenly start feeling the softer side of things. It just doesn't happen.

The tear. I know when I touched it something inside of me changed and Ezekiel confirmed it along with Siren herself. Siren and her magic is making me weak and I have to find a way to avoid her. Maybe that angel is right. Maybe we should just let Siren die. I can't stand the idea of it, but maybe that's why it must happen.

"Are you okay?" Siren suddenly asks me.

"Yes!" I shoot back at her.

She gives me a strange look and rolls her eyes. "Sure you are."

I have to get away from her, the sooner we find this garden or she dies, the better. I will move forward and forget I ever met this magical creature. Fuck, if my father finds out about her, he will surely use her against me. I cannot allow her to get under my skin any more than she has. It has to end now. No more kissing her, although if I get a chance to get into those pants of hers, well who am I to say no to that? Fuck and chuck and that's it. No more of these feelings. The more I think about her spell on me the angrier and angrier I get.

Maybe I should just kill her myself so I can go back to the ruthless demon I was before I met her. I hate her for making me feel all this.

"It's all your fault you know." I snap at Siren.

"What is?" she sounds so confused.

"This!" I say pointing to my chest. "I am feeling emotions because of you and I want it to stop." I growl at her.

"I told you I didn't do anything to you." She shouts at me.

"Your tear." I snarl in her face.

"You never told me when you touched it." She doesn't back down, even a little.

"And I'm not going to, just tell me how I can reverse this magic." I utter murderously quiet.

"I don't know, maybe if I die it will reverse itself." She sounds slightly calmer now.

"Do you know that for a fact?"

"No!" She shakes her head. "I have no idea if my death will change anything, but maybe you will be lucky enough to find out." With that she stomps away from me.

"What the hell is your problem?" Maddy yells at me. "That was completely unnecessary."

"Her magic is changing who I am and you think I'm behaving like what exactly? Irrational maybe?"

"Did she use her magic on you? Did she make you touch her tear? I'm assuming by the fact that she doesn't recall this even happening that the answer is no." She then goes after Siren.

I am going to find a way to reverse this if I have to kill Siren myself. My evilness is necessary to my self-preservation. I cannot afford to feel things for her, to fall in love with her. These things must never happen.

I look around and see that I am in familiar territory, very familiar territory. As in there is a succubus and incubus house up ahead. It's like a strip club with a lot of happy endings due to their nature.

When an immortal creature has sex with one of these creatures, they feel slightly drained of energy, but do not die like might happen with a mortal, and they still get to feed off of it. I know I shouldn't risk being weak, but I really need to get Siren out of my system and if I can't have the real thing, then what better way to do that then to be with a succubus.

"Hey ladies, mind if we stop here?" I point up ahead to the hole in the wall with lots of lights.

"Why would you want to stop there?" Maddy asks disgusted. "Oh, gross."

"What is it?" Siren asks confused.

"It's a cross between what the mortals would call a strip club and a brothel." Maddy answers helpfully.

"Really? You think now is an appropriate time to get your rocks off? Sure, let's stop while I die." Siren sounds down right angry.

"I'll be quick." I remark as I open the door for them.

"No, I wouldn't want to rush you. By all means, take all the time in the world." Siren waves her hand to proceed inside. "Maybe I'll meet an incubus in here." She adds. I do not like the sound of that at all. I clench my fists, but don't take the bait.

"Maybe you will." I try to sound as if this doesn't bother me in the least.

We walk inside a smoky room. People in Hell really like to smoke, and they will smoke anything.

I notice a few succubae are eyeing me up as soon as I walk onto the floor. I am walking toward the stage where they are dancing, all the while they're losing articles of clothing. I notice a few of them licking their lips while giving me a come hither smile. The men near the stage move out of my way and three dancers begin to crowd me. One of them starts kissing my neck while another is nibbling on my earlobe. I feel three sets of hands pawing at me. Two of those sets are rubbing up my chest.

"So, you're going to get laid while Siren gets weaker and weaker?" I hear Maddys voice from right behind me. I don't bother turning around because it's not like I can look her in the eyes anyway.

"Yes, I am going to enjoy these sexy ladies." I won't think of Siren at all while doing it.

"I guess as long as you get off then it doesn't matter if she dies." and she sounds angry.

"Maybe Ezekiel is right." I mutter.

"About?" She sounds determined.

"That it would be better if she did." As soon as the words leave my mouth, I hear a gasp and immediately know that Maddy wasn't there alone. I should have known better. Instead of waiting for what will come next, I put my arms around two of the ladies while the third is waving me to follow with her finger. I need these women to make me forget all about Siren, and I need it now.

(SIREN)

'That it would be better if she did' replays in my mind as I watch Daemon walk away with three floozies. He thinks it would be better if I died. I thought he actually cared about me. I laugh at the thought. How stupid am I? To believe that a creature like him is even capable of caring. I feel this stabbing in my chest. "There is no way that I feel something for that disgusting demon-whore."

"Whoa" Maddy whispers beside me.

"I should have seen that coming." I smile at her in the hopes that she doesn't see the pain behind the mask. The look on her face says that whether she can see it or not, she knows it's there.

"I thought you were the one he wanted." She sounds so shocked that it's almost humorous.

"He's the kind that will take whatever he can get." I shrug it off. "I was just convenient."

"You don't actually believe that do you?" she asks skeptically.

"Yep, seen it plenty. It was my own stupidity to believe for a second that he ever thought about anyone but himself." I feel the ire building, but I try to tamp it down. He. Is. Not. Worth. It.

I go over to the bar and order a drink. I sit there and wait for Mr. I-need-sex-all-the-time-or-else-I'll-die. That doesn't quite roll off the tongue. I guess I'll just call him Mr. Pervy. I sip my drink through my straw and Maddy sits next to me.

"I cannot believe that guy!" she huffs.

"That makes two of us." I sigh while twirling my straw in my drink and watching the ice cubes in my glass. "I think the worst part is that I knew better." I feel so dejected.

"I have seen the way he looks at you. Something is wrong." She sounds pretty adamant for someone who just met the guy, and it wasn't while he was trying to kick some woman out of bed.

"Yeah, in his head. He thinks getting laid is more important than my life." I start twirling the straw so fast that the liquid starts slopping over the sides, so I put down the drink. "I am going to die because he needed a piece of ass."

"We will find the garden Siren. I know we will." She puts her hand on my shoulder in a comforting move.

"I can't believe you would let that thing touch you." I hear someone say from beside me. I look over and flip the guy off. Sometimes no words need to be said. Too bad I feel her hand flinch away from me and then she puts both her hands in her lap. What a twat.

I get up and walk over to the guy "Watch this." I say as I punch him square in the nose. He falls backwards off his stool. I shake out my fist because, damn that hurt. The guy gets up and comes at me. but another one stops him. He looks back at me and I see his eyes change purple and then they are back to a dark brown. Huh, pretty!

I sit back down and turn back to Maddy. "How do you know?" I ask as if nothing happened.

"Know what?" I can tell she has no idea what I'm talking about.

"That we will find the garden. You sound pretty confident."

"I just try to be optimistic when I can be, which is admittedly hard when you live in Hell." I can't argue that logic. I would find it extremely hard to keep a 'can do' attitude if I lived here. "My hand really hurts." I shake it out a little and look at it. My knuckles are turning a purple-blue colour. I have never had a bruise in my life because I heal so quickly, capillaries have nothing on me. I gape at my hand in disbelief.

"That's quite the bruise." Maddy notices my expression as I stare at my hand. I feel real fear about my mortality much stronger than I did before. I can feel a tear threatening to water my eyes so I take a deep breath, hoping that I do not cry in front of all these Hellish creatures. "Oh no, you're bruising." She exclaims.

"Yeah." is all I can choke out. I take a drink right from the glass and chug it back. I don't know what kind it was but it was berrylicious. I just wanted something fruity when I ordered it and man, did they do me right.

"Like I keep saying, we are going to find the garden. We just need to keep looking."

I sigh "What's the point? If I am at the point of bruising like a mortal, than it's just a matter of time before I die." I feel the resignation resonating throughout my body.

"Mind if I sit here?" a man points at the chair beside me.

"Do whatever you want." I sound like a bitch, even to my own ears.

"Want another one?" the guy points at my glass.

"Yes please" I say more upbeat now. The idea of more alcohol sounds like the best idea suggested to me in a long time.

"Are you from around here?" He smiles a charming smile as he asks.

"Hell no." I almost yell but then smile to hide my outburst. "I mean I'm just visiting."

He laughs, shaking his head as if what I said is ludicrous. "Who comes to Hell to visit?" Good point.

"Someone who likes the heat of course." I raise my eyebrow at him as a dare to rebuttal.

"Can't argue that." He takes a drink of, what I can only assume is beer. I know my drink seems stronger than the human brew, I wonder if his is too.

I sit there for a while chatting to the guy when I finally see Daemon come out from the back room with his ladies. His shirt is undone and he looks ruffled. I do not want to talk to him right now. I immediately turn to my new friend... umm... what's his name? I don't think I ever got it. As I look over at him I realize I don't really need to have it, I just need to get out of here and he might be the perfect excuse. I turn to him with the sexiest smile I can manage. "So, want to go somewhere a little quieter?"

He smiles a crooked smile before leaning in toward me. "You sure you know what you're getting yourself into?" Nope, not at all, but I have to leave now.

"The real question is, do you know what you're getting yourself into?" I try to muster all my conviction into that sentence.

"Alright, let's get out of here." He gets off the bar stool and lends me his hand. I grab it and follow him out of the bar. I take a quick peek at Daemon and he looks angry. How dare he be angry at me for wanting to do the same thing that he just did. I need to rid him from my mind and maybe a one night stand will do the trick. This isn't really my cup of tea but I need to get rid of this ache in my chest. In the corner of my eye I see Daemon is rushing toward me at a speed

I didn't know he was capable of. Shit, I must get out of here faster. I am almost dragging the poor guy out the door with me.

"Impatient?" he asks with a smile.

"Very." I say as he grabs me to turn a corner into one of the caves alleyways. It seems like the kind of alley you would see in the human world but a lot more confining due to the nature of a cave. I am walking a little ahead of my new friend when I am suddenly pinned to the wall. I hear a woman chuckle somewhere from behind me.

"What a gift to give our king." Her tone is maniacal. That voice, I recognize that voice. I try to turn my head a little toward where I know she is standing. In my peripheral vision I see her, Gwendolyn. She walks over to where I am pinned and laces her fingers into my hair then bashes my head against the cave wall. Hard. My body goes limp as everything else goes black.

Chapter Sixteen

(Daemon)

Where in Hell is she going? What the Hell does she think she is doing going off alone with some fucking guy? I feel my heart rate accelerate with pure fire in my veins. To say I am seething is an inconceivable understatement. I rush toward her, but she only moves faster with that stupid asshole. She looks back at me briefly and on her face I can see that I am the real reason she is leaving. I don't know what she intends to do with that guy, but I am the one who drove her to do it. Maybe it's a good thing. Maybe now I will be able to keep my distance since it looks like she doesn't want to be anywhere near me.

I follow her out the door, hoping that I can stop her from pursuing whatever it is she wants from him. The guy looks kind of familiar which is never a good sign in my books. My father works with a lot evil creatures down here. As I get out of the strip club, I look both ways trying to gauge where she went. I don't see her anywhere. I walk in one direction, while looking in every other direction that there is, hoping to catch site of her.

The man's face plays over in my head, looking for some kind of recognition. It's up there, I know who that guy is with my Siren. After searching for a block, I stop and lean against a wall breathing heavily. I slam my fist on the wall hard enough that I see a fissure in the rock.

I walk back to the bar and Maddy is standing outside waiting for me. "Did you find her?"

I laugh without humour and it comes out almost like a growl. "Nope, do you know who she was with?"

"No, but I bet someone in there will know who he is." She suggests.

"Alright, let's go back inside."

WE TALK TO A FEW OF the patrons, but a lot of them didn't notice the girl with navy blue hair. How can you not notice something so, well, noticeable?

I go to the bartender who was busy while I did my questioning. "Did you happen to notice a beauty sitting here with navy blue hair and bright blue eyes?"

He smiles at me. "Oh, the one who was sitting with the gorgon earlier?" he notes, pointing at Maddy. "Yeah, she left with some minion of our king. I think his name is Leo."

Leo, that's it, now I remember who he is. He works for my father in his army of evilness. I met him once or twice and even though our encounters were brief, it was obvious that his priority is to please my father. The worst part of this scenario is that he has Siren and I can only imagine what he plans to do with her.

"Are you alright?" I slowly shake my head as I'm lost in a daze full of horror. "Do you know who the guy is?" Maddy asks slowly.

"Yes, and he works for my dad." I choke out the last word. "I think whatever he has planned for Siren has to be full of pain and torture. We need to get her back."

"Okay, but how are we going to get to her?" the poor girl just had to ask.

"Looks like I am going to have to go into the lion's den. You can come if you want to, but I wouldn't recommend it." I don't even want to do this. If I never saw that man again it would be too soon.

"I don't know if there is anything I could do to help, even if I did go with you." She shrugs in a self-deprecating way.

"I understand." I wish I could convey how much I really do. I'm the man's son and I would like nothing more than to avoid him for the rest of eternity. I can't even fathom how she must feel. "I unfortunately need to go now."

"I will stay around here and see if I can find anyone who might know something about the Garden of Eden."

(GWENDOLYN)

I finally have the bitch exactly where I want her. Daemon is never going to choose her over me again and once she is out of the picture I will make my move on him. Oh, this is going to be the most joyous occasion I have encountered in centuries. To watch her bleed and plead for it all to end. I can't wait to start the festivities.

I know our lord will want to take part in some of the pain we are about to wrought. Oh boy, this little girl is going to pray for death by the time we're done with her. I thought she was powerful, she didn't look so powerful in that back alley. I made sure we all drank from that vile her fiancé gave to me, but it looks like it was unnecessary. She didn't even struggle.

I look down at the passed out faery in the dungeon and can't help but cackle. She will be so much fun to play with.

"Are you going to just sit down here and wait for her to wake up?" My lord sneaks up behind me.

"Yeah, I can't wait to cut up that bitch. Maybe I'll even take off a limb or two. So many options." The glee is overwhelming.

"You can have her for a little while, but then it will be my turn. You said Daemon had feelings for her?" Oh, how he would love to hurt anyone close to Daemon. That's why I had to bring her here. She is going to suffer in unimaginable ways.

"Yes, he seemed quite smitten." I can't help the grin that spreads across my face. Not because he was smitten with her, no, that makes me want to cut out her organs, but the fact that she will be out of his life now that is worth grinning about.

"Well, well, well, looks like we have a lot to do then." I don't know where I want to start. I should at the very least have the common decency to wait until she wakes up I suppose. It's not really all that much fun to torture someone if you can't hear their blood curdling screams anyway.

As I'm about to walk away, I hear some quiet moans and I turn around to see Siren's eyes fluttering open.

"Hello Siren." I purr.

"Wha... what's going on?" her tone is groggy. "Ouch." she slowly sits up holding her head, which I can't help but notice still hasn't healed, interesting.

"Looks like you got a bump on the old noggin."

"I think my skull is cracked." She rests her head in both of her hands and moans.

"Ah, I'm sure you will survive the head trauma. It's everything else that might kill you." I chuckle.

That's when she looks up at me. "Uh, I'll be damned." and then she laughs at her joke. "What do you want?" she moans.

"You! Broken!" Oh and broken she will most definitely be.

"Why are you doing this?" Her voice sounds so whiney.

"Because, I can." I laugh. "What are we going to do first?" I ask her while taking out my serrated knife. "What appendages are you the least attached to? A finger? A toe? We'll leave the larger limbs until later."

I see real fear in her eyes now. The kind of fear I'm sure she doesn't feel very often since she was so incredibly powerful. I wonder what happened to her. Oh wait, I don't care.

(SIREN)

I don't know how long I have been here, but whatever the length of time, it feels like an eternity. I can't feel parts of my body, I'm not sure if the nerves have been damaged or if the limbs have been removed completely. I'm afraid to look. Faeries can regenerate, but with this poison in my system I am not sure if that's even an option anymore. I do know that usually I would have healed by now. All this because I had hurt feelings. Was it worth it? Was Daemon worth any of this? Probably not.

I want to move but I'm afraid to. I feel so much wetness on me, sticky wetness. It must be blood. There feels like there is so much of it. I have closed my eyes hoping to block out the pain, plus I really don't need to see that face contort in her lunacy again.

Here I was, afraid I was going to die from a poisoning and here I am possibly being chopped into little bits. Why couldn't I have just allowed the poison to run its course? But no, I had to come to Hell with Daemon. Maybe I would have been safer in Heaven with Ezekiel. To be fair, I don't actually know that he is in Heaven. Wherever he did go though, has to be better than this.

I remember a man. He was very handsome if you like the tall dark and chiselled. His hair was a little on the long side, just covering the tips of his ears, a little shaggy. He had huge black wings that had horns at the tips and dark brown eyes. I remember there were horns that protruded out of his head that had a slight curve toward the back of it. He might have been beautiful on the outside, but is purely ugly on the inside. I thought Gwen had a knack for causing pain, it turns out it was nothing compared to what he could do. Or what else he intends to do. I think he might have said something along the lines of "this is just the beginning."

I feel the darkness again descend.

Chapter Seventeen

(Daemon)

I take a short cut out of the tunnels and into the hot outdoors. Most of the creatures who live down here stay in the tunnels because they can't take the heat and you know what they say, "if you can't take the heat, get out of the fire." I personally think there is more fire down in the tunnels though. There is a hell of a lot more lava down there, pun intended. Now I just have to watch out for those who do live above ground because they are much fiercer for it.

I would use my demonic power to get there, but it's a lot weaker once I'm actually in Hell. Not that I couldn't do it, it would just take a lot more out of me. We can shimmer into the human world which takes a lot of power. Once there though, we can just snap our fingers and get to our destination like nothing. It's some sort of control mechanism so we can't just kill one another for giggles by easily getting the upper hand.

I walk for a good hour when I hear yelling and galloping. Great, just what I didn't want to run into. These have to be the worst to quarrel with because they are the best of hunters. They forge their own weapons out of whatever they can get their hands on. Centaurs!

I look around for something to hide behind, but there really isn't anything of any use to me around here. Boulders? Well they can see over them. Sand? I can't dig a hole fast enough. I guess I'm just going to have to deal with this the best I can.

"Hey, you there." I hear one of them yell.

"Stop right there." another one says.

"Don't even think about it." a female voice adds. They are all surprisingly beautiful for being part horse and all. They all have long dark hair and both males have slightly lighter brown hair about shoulder length. The female has long, almost black hair that just about reaches her horse back. The men are shirtless and are they ever ripped. They put my muscles to shame. The woman who is slightly fairer, but also very muscular has what looks like a light brown leather top that covers her breasts. Probably made out of some poor shmucks hide.

I stop in my tracks and raise my hands in the air to show surrender. They all have their arrows pointed at me and I notice hers is pointed the lowest, somewhere below the belt. I have a feeling I don't want to find out exactly where.

"Where do you think you're going?" one of the males ask.

"I am going to see your lord." I answer in return.

They laugh at the notion "Why would you want to do something like that?" The other man asks, his voice filled with humour.

"Because, he is my father and he has someone I care about."

Their laughter dies and their faces turn serious. "Who is she?" the female asks. At my quirked eyebrow she adds "It has to be a 'she' for you to go through so much trouble."

"She is someone very special to me and that's all you need to know." I sternly state to stop further questioning.

They lower their arrows, which is surprising because they are known for shooting first and asking questions later. Luckily for me they asked first. "Need a lift?" one male asks.

"Are you seriously offering?" I am very skeptical of their suggestion. They aren't known for their hospitality or morality.

"What? Are you scared?" the three of them laugh. "Not all of us are ruthless killers." he confirms some of my beliefs, but...

"So not all of you kill for shits and giggles?"

"Of course not, just most of us do." Well I guess I can take the risk for Sirens sake. After all, I might have had something to do with her taking off with that asshole. The remembrance of seeing her with that man makes my fists and jaw clench, but the thought of what he and my father might be doing to her now makes my heart pick up and my stomach drop.

"I will take the risk... I mean ride. So who wants to carry me?"

The biggest man says, "I'll take you on my back, but the other two will flank me to make sure there are no surprises."

"Sounds good to me."

I HAVE TO ADMIT THAT the ride was a lot faster than doing it by foot. It would have been a long walk and I am going to need as much energy as I can preserve by the time I get to that god forsaken place. I don't know what loops I am going to have to go through, but one thing is for sure, they will not be pretty.

As we get to the gate of the castle, I hear the sound of ballistic dogs barking. Hell hounds, perfect. "Well this is as far as we can go Sir." The centaurs drop me off at the huge gate made of fire. I am not like my father in the sense that I can manifest into a huge living flame, but I do have the power to make it through his flames while only getting horribly burned, I do heal quickly though.

I take a few steps back and run as fast I can through the flaming gate. I found the faster I can run through the fire, the less I am burned. This time I'm red but it doesn't sting much more than a really bad sun burn, so it will heal before I have the displeasure of seeing my dad.

I look around and see a pack of Hell hounds running towards me like they haven't eaten in a while and I'm their best chance at a meal. I really hate Hell hounds. Like any dog they have their loyalties, too bad their loyalties lie in the hands of a sadist.

I create fire balls in my hands and start throwing them at the rabid-like animals. My fire might not be as strong as my fathers, but there is no one else who can compare. All a part of being who I am and who I come from.

I hit one hound and then another and another. Eventually the rest of the pack learned from their fallen comrades and retreated. I really hate Hell hounds.

As I make my way up to the front door, I throw it open and run for the stairs leading down toward the basement. I know exactly where the dungeon is since I have also been locked in there as punishment so many times. I run past the cages with creatures screaming in agony. I look, and in almost every third cage someone is being tortured. Every cage I see some form of gruesome punishment. I move faster, search more urgently. My heart is pounding so hard I think it very well might burst from my chest. Not one of these caged bound beings is Siren.

"You have made it." I hear a familiar feminine voice coming from behind me. I slowly turn around. "Are you going to stay for dinner? It will give us time to catch up."

"Gwendolyn!" I growl. She just smiles and turns around, gesturing with her finger over her shoulder for me to follow. I don't like this one bit.

She leads me to the dining room and the table is set with all the fine dining utensils we have. We don't own fine china down here, but we still have artists that can make the most beautiful pieces. There are candles lit in the middle to add a certain kind of mood. Knowing my father, the mood is 'terrified' or 'I wish I was dead, please stop'. That one's my favourite. My father is at the head of the table and he only nods his head for me to sit down.

"I'm glad you made it son."

"What are you up to?" I know this man is scheming.

He doesn't say a word, only takes the lid off of the first platter and takes a healthy helping of whatever it is inside. With him you can never be too sure. A man comes in with a huge cupboard on wheels and pushes it into the room. He turns it toward us.

"Dinner and a show." My father says with a grin that makes me sick to my stomach. The doors open and inside is Siren, chained to the back of the case and she is bleeding profusely. She opens her eyes and sees me and then closes them again.

"Isn't this wonderful?" Gwendolyn squeals while clapping her hands like a small child who is waiting to be given the biggest present she has ever seen. I feel my stomach flip. Siren has lost too much blood, her skin is so pale it's almost blue, but I can see that her wounds are starting to coagulate. She is such a mess of blood and destroyed flesh that I can't even see how bad the damage actually is.

My father gets up and walks over to me. "You are going to finish her off."

"No, I can't do that." My heart is beating so hard in my chest that I can't even catch my breath. This cannot be happening. I didn't want this to happen. Siren's eyes pop open and she watches me.

"You can and you will." My father walks over to a drawer under the cupboard or wardrobe like thing Siren is in. In the drawers is an assortment of weapons for me to choose from.

"Do it Abaddon." A name I haven't heard in a very long time. In more than one millennia.

"Abaddon?" Siren says in a quiet and scratchy voice.

"KILL HER!" My father yells.

"I won't do it." I say pleadingly. I feel a sob in my throat and swallow the lump. It will do no good for me here.

"What is this? Do you love her?" My dad chuckles his cruel chuckle.

"Of course not." I peek at Siren and she looks so broken and scared. It's heartbreaking.

"Then you should have no trouble killing her!" My father looks angry. It's like being a child all over again as my father hurts those I love in order to punish me. When hurting them wasn't satisfying anymore he escalated, but this, this is the worst I have ever seen.

I stand up "NEVER!" I shout.

"Fine, I will." My father walks over to her and before I can even think, he lights her on fire using only his demonic powers. I run, taking off my clothes and using them to put her out.

"Good show Lord Diablos." Gwendolyn says from the table eating what looks like an overgrown chicken leg. I don't want to know who that leg belonged to. My father really is the devil, in every sense of the word. After I put out the fire, I hold Siren and use my demonic powers to get her to my home. I know it will be safe. Her injuries are so severe I don't think she will even make it through the night. This is all my fault.

(MADDY)

I have wandered around inquiring about the garden to no avail. I sit here at the bar waiting for Daemon. I have given up hope that any of these monsters will be able to help me.

Someone walks into the bar and everything goes silent except for the sound of a few gasps. I turn to see what all the lack of commotion is about when I see him. One of the most beautiful men I have ever seen. Tall with dark brown hair and green eyes with a gold ring around them. I have never seen one before, but even without seeing his wings I can tell that he must be a holy angel. A beautiful, magnificent angel. Oh and he is walking straight for me. I wish I could say he was staring right at me, but if he were we would all know it as he turned into a beautiful and magnificent statue.

"Are you the gorgon that was with Daemon and Siren?" he asks. Well, it's nice for him to get straight to the point. None of those pesky pleasantries.

"Um, yes?" I know it came out as a question, but I don't know this guy.

"Are you not sure?" His voice is melodic and oh so stern.

"Yes, I was with them. And you would be?"

"Ezekiel and I have been trying to catch up to them. Do you know where they are?" Maybe he can help somehow.

"Daemon's father has Siren." And who knows what he is doing to her as we speak.

"Shit, okay. What do you know thus far?" Are all angels so authoritative?

"I know that Siren is captured by the worst of the worst and that Daemon went to save her. I haven't heard from either of them since they left and I haven't found any information on what they seek." I huff out.

"I might be able to help with the latter." He nods. "I know that the garden is down here and even though I don't know its exact location, I was told that Hell was created because of the garden. If that is the case then it must be somewhere in the centre. Now we just have to find out where that point might be."

"It must be above ground then." She nods in thought.

"I would assume so, yes." Huh, all I had to do for information was wait for this handsome stranger.

"Now what do we do about Daemon and Siren?" There is a chance we might not have to find the garden if anything happens to her.

"I have no idea." The angel sounds a little perplexed. He suddenly brightens up. "If she was injured he would take her to a place he knew was safe, his home." Of course he would.

"We don't know where that is though."

"Ah, a popular demon's son? I think we can figure it out, ask around."

Good idea angel boy... man. The angel turns around and faces the crowd and says with great volume and yet without actually yelling "Does anyone know where Daemon might live?"

The crowd is silent for a moment when a couple hands go up in the air. Of course they are mostly women.

"I have been there." A beautiful and voluptuous woman says and I can definitely see the allure. He gestures for her to continue. "If you go straight through the tunnels and then turn left at the first turn and then you continue down there until you see steps that go up to the surface, and half way up them there will be a door. That's his place. Part of his house breaks through above ground." That was very descriptive.

"You know the place well?" Ezekiel asks.

"Oh yeah!" She has a smug smile.

"Thank you for the help, it was much appreciated." Ezekiel says to her. "Let's go get them." he whispers to me.

Chapter Eighteen

(Siren)

I am strung up like a hunter's carcass with wounds I'm not sure I could ever heal from and I see Daemon. He looks mortified and like he might be sick.

The evil man I have heard referred to as Lord Diablos just called Daemon Abaddon. Abaddon? Maybe he wasn't talking to him, or maybe I'm delirious from the blood loss and pain. Daemon refused to put me out of my misery. At this point it would be a blessing.

The evil man shoots a bright flaming light at me and I feel it burn so immensely, in a way I never would have thought possible. It feels like my skin is melting if that is even possible.

I wake up and realize the pain from my dream has been carried over to real life and I try to move but I can't. I remember that the events from my dream are actually memories. Horrifying memories that somehow I seem to have survived. I wish I didn't because I am going to suffer though a painful healing process and then die anyway. What kind of justice is that?

I feel like my entire body is wrapped up, and if that's true it's probably gauze to stop anything from getting into the open wounds that I used to call my body. My entire body. I feel the pain take over and I am out again.

I wake up again from the same traumatizing nightmare of my life and almost death, and the pain I wake up too is still paralyzing. I feel that someone is tending to my wounds, and I try to open my eyes. I see Daemon leaning over me and he looks as if he's concentrating hard on his work. I move my fingers.

"Shh," Daemon whispers soothingly. "You don't want to move much now."

I turn my head and in my peripheral vision I see what looks like raw meat for an arm. I gasp and then choke which is extremely painful for both my smoke damaged lungs and my charcoaled skin. Again blackness greets me.

I wake up to other familiar voices. It sounds like Maddy and Ezekiel but I can't be sure. They sound panicked as if they just saw the most terrifying thing imaginable. I guess they looked at me. I have no idea how long I have been out for. Hours? Days? Weeks? All I know for sure, is that I am not healing very quickly, which means the poison has compromised my system too much. I'm dead regardless.

"Siren?" I hear Maddy's voice. I wish I could look at her, but even if I was able to see her, I still couldn't. "I am so sorry this happened to you. No one deserves this, well except for the one who did this." She sounds so devastated.

"I didn't think she was going to make it." I hear Daemon's voice. "The way she looked after I put out the flames, I will never forget that, no matter how hard I try." He sounds sorrowful and it takes me aback a little.

"That must have been hard to see." Maddy agrees.

"I know this is my fault. I said some awful things to her the other day, it was because of this that I said them." What? Because of this? What does that even mean?

"What do you mean, because of this?" Thank you Maddy for asking the questions I cannot.

"My father loves nothing more than to hurt those close to me in the most foul of means." Daemon's voice has a darkness I have never really heard before. "This is my fault for so many reasons and all because my dad would love to hurt those I care about. I pushed her away and then she left with that male who lured her into this. All because of me." I hear a hard thump.

"You couldn't have known all this would happen to her." Maddy sounds consoling.

"You should have known." Ezekiel sounds livid. "He's your father and all things evil." His voice is getting louder. "You are a demon and I seem to have forgotten that you are just like him. How do we know that you didn't have any part in this?"

I hear a growl and it could have only come from Daemon. "You have no idea what I had endured growing up. My father made me into a monster by maiming everyone I ever cared about..." he takes a deep breath and lowers his voice. "Including my mother."

Ouch! What? Daemon's father killed his mother?

"I recently realized that my feelings for her were going to get her killed." Daemon stops for a second and I can feel his eyes on me. "Now I also know that seeing her die will kill me, so I have to keep my distance."

"So you aren't even going to try to make things work with her?" Maddy sounds indignant.

"If I don't let her go she will die." I hear another thump. "I might get the pleasure of seeing that anyway. She isn't fucking healing. It has been days and I see such little progress."

"Do you think she's going to make it?" Maddy asks.

"Honestly? I have no idea. Even if she does, I don't think we have enough time to find the garden." Daemon sounds pained.

"We can at least make her comfortable as the mortals say." Ezekiel adds.

They don't think I'm going to make it. Really, am I surprised? I don't even think I will. How can I blame them for just saying it out loud? I feel a tear run down my cheek. I'm going to die and I'll be living out my last days burnt to a crisp. How is this even fair?

"What are you doing?" Maddy asks.

"What is that?" Ezekiel asks at the same time.

"This is a lovely plant I found above ground. It grows around my house and all she has to do is sniff it and she will be out again. I smell something weird and everything else fades away.

I HEAR SOBBING AND whispering and it wakes me from a more peaceful slumber.

"I am so sorry this happened to you. I would do anything to see you're pretty face, even if you hated me for pushing you away. If you knew how much I loved you, how much I need you to live, you wouldn't blame me for what I did." I hear Daemon breathing heavily as if trying to stop the crying.

"Seeing you burned was by far the worst pain I have felt in my very long life. Trust me when I say I have suffered through a lot of pain." He whispers the last part.

I want to hold him through his sorrow but there is literally nothing I can do right now.

"I don't know if I can stand the thought of being here when you die, but the thought of leaving is unbearable." He sniffs. "I am going to be so lost." Whoa, I didn't see this confession coming at all. I feel a light kiss on my lips and then I hear him leave.

The next time when I wake up, I feel strange. I turn my head and realize that my skin has somewhat knit back together. Ah, that weird sensation? Is it lack of pain? Not that I don't still hurt, but I think I can actually move now. I slowly sit up just to fall back down. "Ouch!" Okay, I can't sit up, but only because my muscles feel seriously unused. I hear feet thumping across the floor.

"Siren?" Daemon runs into the room and to the side of my bed. "I am so happy to see that you're doing better that I could hug you." He scrutinizes my body. "Maybe not yet though."

"Can we go find the garden?" I ask desperately.

"You are in no condition to do that Siren." Daemon reprimands.

"I don't have much time so let's just do this. I would rather die trying then to live another moment in this stupid bed." My voice is a little scratchy but I think I made my point clear.

"Okay." He sighs. "We will leave soon so get ready!" He leaves and closes the door. I hear him yell "Up everyone, Siren is awake and wants to find the garden, we are leaving in thirty minutes".

I get out of bed and nearly fall, but I catch myself on the bedside table. Okay, I can do this. I take a few more steps, willing myself not to fall. I put my arms out like an aeroplane for balance. It didn't really help me when my knees gave out and I fell to the floor, hard.

"Siren are you okay?" Maddy asks as Ezekiel comes over to help me up.

"Yeah, just learning how to walk." I laugh it off even though I really bruised my pride. And my rear.

WE HAVE BEEN WALKING for hours in the blistering heat of Hell. The sun is burning my already charred skin. It has healed to a blistering, scabbing state. It hurts like hell, but it's probably better than the exposed nerve state that I am happy I was unconscious for. Mind you this state kind of feels like my nerves are exposed. As we walk I feel the ground shake.

"Shit!" Daemon says.

"Shit?" Ezekiel asks. "Shit what?"

"Is it an earthquake, or I guess in this case a Hellquake? This time I am the one to ask the question. I have this gnawing feeling that it's something bad.

"It's a Hell worm." Daemon finally answers.

"A worm? I think we can take a worm." I laugh. The earth shakes again. "How big is this worm?"

"Let's just keep walking." Daemon turns and continues while speeding up his pace.

"Why are you walking so fast?" I chase after him, along with Ezekiel and Maddy. I hear a shrill sound from behind me and turn around just in time to see a huge worm diving into the sand similar to a dolphin.

"Uh, let's walk faster" I say, moving to an almost run.

"No, it's like any wild animal when it's comes to their prey. They enjoy the chase." Daemon grabs my hand and pulls me back. I feel a rippling under my feet and come to a halt. The worm comes out of the ground and its face is suddenly in mine. It shrieks again and I see that its mouth opens on four sides that comes to a point at the end. It actually reminds me of the paper fortune teller game I saw some kids playing at the homeless shelter. I take a deep breath trying to tamp down my fear.

"Don't move." Daemon whispers. There is seriously no fear of that. Whoa, I never understood what real fear feels like because I was stronger and more powerful than most. Since I have been poisoned I have felt little else.

Before I can really comprehend the situation, I see its head fall to the ground with the rest of its body following. I turn to see Ezekiel cleaning off his sword. "That didn't seem so scary."

"Well then, may we continue?" Maddy says with a slightly shaken tone.

AFTER A WHILE OF SILENCE, memories come streaming back to me. Some of them are replays of memories that keep going through my head on repeat, but some of them are new ones. After all the shock of everything, I forgot some of the reasons why I ended up in that state. I remember Daemon leaving with the women, and that he said it would be better if I died. I feel the residual sting. I remember a little bit between the torture and the torching. Particularly the part where Daemon is being told by this evil man to kill me. Daemon called him father and... the evil man called him... something. What was it? Abe? Abaddon? Yes, that's it, Abaddon.

"Who is Abaddon?" Daemon stiffens, but doesn't answer.

"Your, um, father called you that, did he not?" He doesn't look at me, but keeps his eyes up ahead. Silence.

"He was your father wasn't he?" Still nothing.

I give up. He obviously isn't going to say anything. We walk a while in silence, and no one else seems inclined to fill it. We walk and we walk in the hot desert like (only worse) sun.

"My name is Abaddon." Daemon mutters, suddenly breaking the silence. "When I was little, my father couldn't stand having a soft demon as a child. I wanted to be an angel so bad, to do good things, but my father never would have allowed it. He took me out to kill, maim and torture and I couldn't do it. I couldn't do it until my father made me.

"He would chain me up and torture me, then he started hurting people I loved. He killed many of them too. I became the worse kind of demon because I had to. I had to remind myself that this is who I am, and I can never be anything else, because those I care about will always get hurt. Always pay for it. He called me Daemon as a reminder of my weakness, I kept it as a reminder that I can never be weak again."

I feel a tear stream down my face at the heartbreaking story. I don't even know how to respond to that. I mean, what can you even say to that?

"I never knew." Ezekiel says. "I guess I just assumed, like father like son."

"I know, everyone always does." Daemon's response is filled with Melancholy. "You know the funny part? I didn't even sell my soul so to speak, until my father killed my mother. She was the one who encouraged me to be who I was. She was a fallen angel. Not all of them are evil, they just did something that the higher power considered rebellious, and were cast out of heaven. That's all."

"Oh Daemon... Abaddon, I'm so sorry." I finally choke out. No wonder he seemed so careless. It would be hard to care about anything if it would just be taken away from you in the worst way possible, by one of the people who are always supposed to love and cherish you. I thought my parents were terrible.

"Don't ever call me that." Daemon snarls at me.

I'm so taken aback, I can't even muster up an apology. The instant regret in his eyes speaks volumes. I just hope he can see the regret in mine as well.

"Abaddon is long dead and Daemon is all I will ever be."

"Well Daemon, there is definitely something good inside of you." I whisper, hoping I don't set him off.

"How can you of all people believe that?" Daemon sounds angry now. "Look at what I did to you. If I didn't go off with those... If I didn't leave you, then maybe I could have protected you."

I feel my heart break at the memory. I don't say anything because he isn't completely wrong. He isn't right either though. It's not like he could have fathomed that would have happened.

"You couldn't have known." Ezekiel is the one to respond to him.

"But I suspected it would happen eventually." Daemon snaps back.

"Yet those succubae were worth more than Siren." Maddy says in a tone that has all of us turning our heads to look at her, luckily we all stop before we make eye contact, forgetting momentarily of the repercussions. "You just needed a piece of ass, but at whose expense?" She hisses even angrier.

"I don't ever have to explain myself to you. Any of you." and then he storms off ahead of us. "I'm going to help Siren find this garden, and then I am out of here." He throws over his shoulder.

"Whoa" I mouth to Maddy and Ezekiel. They both nod their agreement.

(DAEMON)

Maddy has no idea what she's talking about. I had my reasons for doing what I did, and she will never understand them. I am who I am because my father made me this way. Because my father was a monster.

Every time I look at Siren, I want to touch her and kiss her. Anything to be close to her. Then I remember what it was like when I thought she was going to die, and the previous thoughts wither and die. The memory of my father burning her alive is enough to turn anyone away. I don't know how I will live through Siren's death and as much as I hope she doesn't die, realistically, no one really knows where the garden is. We are going off speculation which is the only thing we have. That doesn't seem so promising.

I know on some level, Siren might never give me another chance and honestly, I don't deserve one. By my need to protect her, I inadvertently put her in danger. I can't say one way or the other if I could have saved her from all this had I not left her alone and gone off with the sexy ladies. I couldn't even go through with it either. All I thought about when I was with them, and they were stripping me down was that they weren't Siren. I am so screwed... figuratively speaking of course. I ended up pushing them off me and putting my clothes back on. By the time I got out of there though, Siren was already rushing away.

I look over at her now. Seeing her blistered skin is a constant reminder that I will never be good enough for her. Live or die, I am going to lose her.

"So, he got laid at the first opportunity?" Ezekiel asks Siren. "It's a known fact that he's a whore." I see in the corner of my eye that he is suddenly walking very close to her. Is he kidding me right now?

"Yeah, I knew that too. I could after all hear his endeavours through the door, and I still believed...." She doesn't finish her sentence. "I just thought maybe he had more respect for me is all." Siren declares instead.

"He's an idiot to give up someone like you." Ezekiel murmurs soothingly.

"Puh-lease. You came at me with a sword." I feel a little relief with her counter. I know she deserves someone better than me, but it will never stop me from wanting her. And I do want her. I just know that no good will come from that.

"I was jealous. I saw you talking to Daemon when I was forming feelings for you. In hindsight, I may have overreacted." Nice save asshole.

"Why?" Siren questions.

"Way to show her you care." Maddy adds.

"If you saw how powerful she was, you might not be so excepting either. I saw the damage she could do to a man without even touching him." He says pointedly to Maddy. "But once I got to know her, I also saw another side, a soft and sweet side. One that gave to the needy." I can see his fondness of her as he looks back at Siren. That sweet talking piece of shit.

"I wish someone would look at me like that." Maddy says on a sigh. "Or at all." Her tone is more sombre.

"Oh Maddy," Siren begins. "You did hear the part where he wanted to kill me right?" I can hear a bit of laughter in her voice. She is an odd duck.

"Because he wanted you so much that he was jealous. It's kind of romantic." Maddy tries to declare.

"Yeah, having a sword drawn on you is kind of romantic. He's just lucky I didn't light him on fire to add a little ambiance." Now I like the way Siren thinks. I can't help but chuckle under my breath.

"I am sorry for what I did." I have no idea what Ezekiel is trying pull here.

"Yeah, well you did tell Daemon I was better off dead so..." Ouch, that burn makes the fires of hell seem cold. The angel doesn't say a damn thing. Good.

Maddy just gasps. I guess she didn't realize it was him who said it first. I can't believe I was the one who said that to Siren though. The look on her face was absolutely stricken. And I did that.

"At least he wanted you." Maddy whispers. I can't imagine what it's like being a girl that no man will ever be able to look at. To never be told she is beautiful. Whoa. I have never felt this... what is it? Empathy? Yuuuck! Wait, was there a double entendre there? Is it possible she could have a crush on him? Nah!

I hear Siren cough, nothing serious, but it definitely sounded like it came from deep down.

"Are you okay there?" I ask concerned.

"Yeah, I think so." is her reply.

We make it a little further when she coughs again. This time much harder.

Seriously Siren, are you okay to keep going?" I ask again.

"That didn't sound good." Ezekiel agrees.

"The sooner I make it to the garden, the sooner I will be back to myself." She keeps walking, like a woman on a mission, before having another coughing fit.

This time she looks at me with fear in her eyes. I run over to her as she collapses onto her knees. "Siren." is all I can get out.

"I. Can't. Breathe" she says as she wheezes out the words. She is trying to breathe as she's on her hands and knees, gasping for air. And there isn't a damn thing I can do to help her.

"Every...thing....is...going...black." she gasps out. She coughs and blood splatters the ground, right before her arms and legs give out from under her and she collapses onto the ground. I hope she's not dead.

I run over to her. "Siren? Wake up." I turn her onto her back. Her lips have a blue hue to them, her skin is so pale it's not far behind. I check her pulse and it's weak. It might be weak, but at least it's there.

Maddy and Ezekiel kneel next to me beside her. "What are we going to do? Will she even make it to the garden?" Maddy asks.

I feel my throat tighten at the same time that dust enters my eye making me tear up. Demons don't cry. "I have no idea, but I'll carry her." I demand. There is no way I want that angel pawing her. Or anywhere near her really.

I pick her up but she's completely limp. It's weird seeing this vibrant and strong woman so weak and vulnerable. She is so beautiful, even still.

"We don't have much time for error looking for this garden of Hell." I spit while rushing forward, not knowing if I am walking in the right direction or just walking further and further away.

"I don't want to lose her either." Maddy says forlornly. "I really hope you know where you're going Ezekiel."

"I can't be sure, but it would make sense if the garden is here in Hell." Hopefully he's as confident as he sounds.

Chapter Nineteen

(Daemon)

We walk for another couple hours as Siren's heart gets weaker and weaker. I constantly check her pulse to make sure she's still alive. About twenty minutes ago, I felt panic surge as I had to search for her pulse and had great trouble finding it. It was so weak that she could die at any second.

"This place looks a little different from the rest of Hell." I observe.

"I was just thinking the same thing." Maddy agrees. "There is shrubbery here, but it looks pretty dead." She adds.

"Yeah, but it's so dry here that these plants shouldn't even be here unless..." Ezekiel gets on his knees and starts digging a hole in the dirt and sand. He doesn't have to dig too deep before we start seeing that the dirt is moist. A little deeper and there is a small puddle of water. "I think we found it." Ezekiel smiles with glee. "Lay her down here and put her hand in the water."

"Are you sure this is the right place? It doesn't look magical to me unless things that look magical, also look dried up, shrivelled and dead." I lie her down anyway, sincerely hoping we found the right place, and put her hand in the small hole Ezekiel dug out. Nothing seems to be happening.

"Is there any change?" Maddy asks.

"I don't think so." I reply.

"Look!" Ezekiel points at Siren whose skin has a slight shine to it. I notice that the dead plants are brown, but looking less dead. The water starts to rise upwards from the hole in the ground.

"What's happening?" Maddy stumbles back a couple steps.

"I have no idea" I mumble.

Her skin starts to glow brighter and the shrubs get greener and greener, taller and taller. The dirt and sand that the ground is made of becomes grassy. The water in the hole hiccups before flooding, rapidly becoming a stream.

Siren doesn't just glow with her natural beauty, I see a glow around her being absorbed by her body. The greenery gets greener still. Some of the shrubs have grown into huge trees that look like they're millions of years old by their girth. As the water rises, Siren looks healthier and the greenery spreads throughout Hell.

I look around, realizing that the desert we were in merely minutes ago has grown over, turning into a forest with this garden in the middle that's both beautiful and plentiful. So many flowers of all different shapes and colours surround us.

"This looks like how I would imagine Heaven to be." Maddy whispers.

"This is far more beautiful." Ezekiel whispers back.

"You ssss-saved the garden." A voice comes from behind us. I turn to see a serpent slithering toward us. A huge, ugly snake.

"Looks like she has." I point my head in Sirens direction.

"Ssss-she looks like ssss-she was poisss-oned." The snake hisses.

"Yeah by basilisk poison." I tell him.

"Oh... sss-she was-ssss lucky to live long enough to find the garden." The snake slithers toward us. "I know of a creature whos-ssse venom is greater than the basilisks, if you can get close enough to find her."

"What is it, and where can we find it?" I ask.

"In the world where the Gods-ss and Goddess-ssesss are trapped. Down in the Underworld isss where Hydra lives-sss."

"Wait, Gods and Goddesses? Underworld? Hydra? I thought that they were all lore." Ezekiel pipes up.

"Yet you jus-ssst sss-saved a faery." The three of us look at each other in agreement. The snake has a valid point. "Hydra is-sss at the gate to the Underworld making sure no one can get in and that no one, God or beast alike, can get out."

"Who are these Gods and Goddesses?" Ezekiel sounds pissed.

"Guess-sss"

"There is only one true God." The angel is getting worked up over the fact that he could have been wrong for his entire existence.

"If you sss-say sss-so." The snake hisses out.

"What happened?" Siren groans as her eyes flutter open.

"We found the garden." I tell her.

She looks around in wonder before holding out her hand for me to help her out of the now pool of water that is beginning to look more and more like a huge pond. Just as I pull Siren out of the water, Maddy jumps in. It's not long before she's screaming in agony as we pull her out carefully, without looking into her eyes. She has blisters all over her body.

"The garden can do many things-sss, but ridding a cursss-se by a Goddess-sss isss-sn't one of them. You need to find Athena." The snake says as he starts slithering away. "Don't let the faery kill Hydra for she is-sss what keeps-sss all the beings-sss trapped down there."

"How do we find the Underworld?" I call after it.

"You will find the ansss-swersss you sss-seek here in the garden." He continues on his way, leaving us to decipher what in Hell he meant.

"Are you okay?" Siren asks Maddy, who looks like she is in agony.

"I really hoped that would cure me from this ugliness." Maddy answers, sounding more depressed and agonized than before.

"Well, you can always look for Athena." I try to add helpfully, but the look I receive from Siren says it wasn't helpful at all.

"Yeah, let's go find a Greek Goddess who may or may not exist in the first place. Yeah, no problem." Maddy's tone is extremely aggravated.

"If that was the serpent of the garden, which I do believe it was, he might know what he's talking about on this one." I can't help pointing out.

"Yeah, if we go to the underworld where the Gods and Goddesses are, we will find Hydra." She says clearly pondering what I just pointed out.

"Hydra?" Siren gasps out.

"Yeah. The snake said she could be used for vengeance." I say with glee.

"In myth she is extremely poisonous, but also extremely hard to get close to." Siren points out enthusiastically.

"You have heard of Hydra?" Maddy sounds astounded.

"You have heard of faeries right?" Siren rebuttals.

"True enough." Maddy sighs.

"So, anyone know where this Underworld is?" Siren calls out to us excitedly.

"No, but the snake said we could find everything we need to know in here." I shrug.

"Where?" Siren spins around.

"I have absolutely no idea." I shake my head while looking at the rest of the garden. It's actually quite big. Although most of it is pretty open, there are bushes and trees within it and aound the garden is a forest. As I look at it I realize that it isn't very thick which is very easy for walking. There is one tree just outside the garden that is massive in comparison to the others around it. I slowly walk towards it.

"Whoa, that tree is massive." Maddy says from behind me.

"It looks like there's a hole in it." Siren cocks her head as she stares at its enormous trunk. She walks forward and then is gone from sight.

(SIREN)

I walk inside the tree and it's incredibly dark. Oh yeah, I have my magic back. I lift my hands and create little twinkling lights right above my head. I really missed my magic. I wonder how I got it back, I bet Vulcan is seething right now. Oh well!

I look around at what was the dark space and I see what looks like a staircase going down. As in way, way down. It's actually kind of fancy looking.

I walk to the top of the stairs and see that it winds down. To where? I can't tell you because I cannot see the bottom. I look back in the direction I entered and I see light from outside. It's not shining in though. In fact, it's like a hazy sheet is set over the doorway, blocking everything on the outside.

I walk back to the door and reach my hand out, testing out the barrier. Someone grabs my hand and yanks me out of the tree and into a hard broad chest.

"Ouch! What do you think you're doing?" I look up and see Daemon looking down at me, worry in his eyes.

"You disappeared Siren." He studies me for a moment before looking into my eyes. His softens and he gently caresses my face. "I didn't know what happened to you."

"I don't know either. I just walked in that hole in the tree." I point toward the tree.

"What hole?" He looks at the tree, scrutinizing it.

"The almost human size one right in front of your face."

"It's not that I don't believe you Siren, it's that I don't see it."

"I don't either." Ezekiel says from behind us.

"Follow me if you can." I say as I drag Daemon toward the tree. "Maddy, you are in no condition to follow, I think you should stay here." I feel bad saying that to her but luckily she agrees. The three of us manage to fit inside. I look at the staircase and nod at it with my head. "Shall we?"

"We shall." Daemon starts walking ahead.

WE WALK AND WALK AND walk down the stairs. They spiral and spiral into the depths that leads to, well, who really knows. Personally I'm hoping it's the Underworld. It looks promising from what I can't see, it's dark and ominous in appearance. Finally we get to the bottom and again I see light coming from the outside but it refuses to illuminate anything inside this dark hole. We slowly retreat through the hole and through to the other side.

It's foggy. As I looked around, I noticed that even though it was night time, I can see my surroundings with clarity. With a look to the sky, I note the huge radiant full moon. Honestly, our surroundings remind me of a grave yard in every horror movie. The fog, the full moon and the leafless trees that look rickety. The only thing missing is the tombstones. Even though there are trees, most of the area seems meadow like.

I listen and I hear what sounds like an angry river bashing against the rocks. I look at the other two and notice they are all doing the same thing... looking at each other.

We slowly descend upon the river, not knowing what to expect from our surroundings. The water looks angry as it flows downstream.

"I have a bad feeling about this." I mumble, mostly to myself.

"You and me both." Ezekiel says back. I don't even know how he heard me with the sound of the running water.

We walk closer yet, trying to decide where we should go and if we should follow the river. Well, I was, I don't know about the other two.

I see something in the water. "What was that?" I point.

"What?" Daemon is looking out for any abnormality, you can tell he is unsure about what he may find.

"Never mind, it might have been all in my head." I shake it off. Must have been imagining things. Looking out, I see it again. "There!" I say pointing again.

"What was that?" Ezekiel takes a step back.

Daemon, being the brave one of the bunch, takes a couple of steps closer. He peaks into the river when something huge lunges up at him. He stumbles backwards before it can take hold of him. The creature looks like a huge serpent, what's on top is truly alarming. One, two, three, four, five, six... A lot of heads. I couldn't count them all because I realized, while I was doing that, I was distracted. With that many heads, I can't let my one head be unfocused.

It lungs toward Ezekiel but he is quick at drawing his sword and takes off its head. In its place, two more grow back. I realized all too late that, shit, this might be Hydra. I don't know why I didn't realize it right off the hop. I mean, who else has that many heads? That many really angry heads with revenge and hunger in all those eyes. I mean, I can't say for sure all the eyes look that terrifying, just the eight or so in my direct line of vision.

One of the heads lunge at me and I twirl out of the way in the nick of time. I materialize a sword and I am ready for the next lunge. I hate to say that I did it, but I did, I cut off another head knowing two more would grow. This creature has grown quite a few heads just since we have been here which makes me wonder... how many times has someone cut off a head? Did Hydra start off with one head? Shit, she's lunging again. All we need is the venom, so why aren't we going for the severed heads?

I look around for just that when I see one. I run towards it, but I see flames coming from Hydra's direction. It just misses me, but the head is charred. Okay, not only does it have one of the strongest of venoms, but it also vomits flames. Something to remember.

After the fighting, the repeated decapitation and not to mention almost being barbecued, we decided to get the hell out of there, don't mind the pun. We rush back towards the tree when Ezekiel and Daemon stop abruptly in front of it. I take their hands and pull them toward the opening that apparently only I can see. We run up the stairs and come out in the Garden of Eden. All of us breathing heavily and sitting down on the grass, clearly exhausted.

"So how much does the gorgon mean to you?" I hear both a familiar and loathed voice say from behind us.

Chapter Twenty

(Siren)

The first thing I saw when I got out of the tree to the underworld is the bitch from hell. Literally, not figuratively. Yes it was Gwendolyn and she was holding her sword over a very unconscious Maddy. One slip and there goes Maddy's head. I look at the gorgon and realize three things simultaneously. First of all, not even Maddy's snakes are moving. Second, I have not been turned to stone and third, the gorgon is rather beautiful. Small nose, symmetrical features, high cheek bones and full lush lips. Basically, any woman would envy her.

"What have you done?" I ask in sheer horror. Please tell me you didn't kill her.

"She was like this when I got here. It's pretty easy to sneak up on a passed out gorgon." Gwendolyn looks down in faux pity at my friend. "Looks like I would be doing the poor dear a favour by putting her out of her misery." She cackles. Yes cackles, and the sound makes my ears want to bleed.

"What did you ever see in her?" I turn to Daemon.

He shrugs. "Easy lay." Right, total horndog.

"Really, is that the only reason? I do believe we had centuries of love making." She looks over at me and grins.

"Ah, you thought it was love until one day he got bored and left." I nod as if I know those are the facts. I don't, but it seems plausible enough.

"You know nothing." She points the sword towards me. Better than Maddy. She addresses Daemon. "Are you not worried that she is the bearer of your prophesy?" She quirks her brow mockingly. I hate her almost as much as I hate the man who poisoned me.

"Prophesy?" I snort which was rather unladylike, even for me.

"About the woman who will destroy him?" She adds.

"Lady, if I was going to destroy him, I would have done it months ago." I see Daemon nod in my peripheral.

"Maybe she is waiting for a more opportune time." She suggests to him.

"Maybe, but I am willing to take my chances. Now can you back away from our friend?" He asks far too politely. I look over at him and can tell that there is forbearing. His jaw is tense and I see muscles twitching that I have never seen twitch before.

"What do you care if I hurt this... this thing?" She shrieks.

"Let's say I don't, but what about what you did to Siren?" His voice is as smooth as silk. Murderously smooth.

"Oh her? I was trying to save you." She sounds flippant, but her eyes have fear in them.

"Yes her." He snarls. I can't decide if he's scary when he's angry or really hot. Maybe both? I can't think about that right now.

"This time I am going to make sure I kill her." She all but growls. Daemon takes a step in front of me but I lightly push him out of the way.

"You think so?" I say sugary sweet. She throws a fire ball at me. I blow air through my lips and the fire turns into dust. I look at her with a 'cat ate the canary' look. In this situation, I am most definitely the cat. She starts wielding her sword and showing off her skill. She must have forgotten I'm a faerie, we don't need skill, plus we're magical creatures who are far more superior to a lowly demon.

"I don't know why you won't just die." The look in her eyes is lethal. If I were anyone else, I might be terrified. Now I just feel mortified, for her of course. "When I'm done with you however, you will wish you did."

"If basilisk poison couldn't take me down, and being tortured and burned couldn't do it, what makes you think that you can?" Now I'm just goading her. I feel Daemon reach for my shoulder, but I shake him off.

Gwendolyn swipes the sword at my neck and I duck mere seconds before it takes off my head. I reach out my hand and grab out her heart. She stumbles backwards in shear shock. I add some of my tears to it and put it back into her body. All before she is able to pull herself together.

"I believe I'll let you live." I smile brightly at her. "Some things are worse than death."

"What did you do?" She whispers.

"Made you a reflection of all your past deeds. Have fun living an eternity with them." She falls to her knees and starts to sob. After Daemon picks up Maddy, I am able to prance away from her guiltlessly. Yes, I pranced, it felt warranted.

Once we were away from the scene of the crime, I turn to Daemon and Ezekiel. "You two should take her back to Xavier, I have a gut feeling that he will take care of her. I will go to my land and get a siren."

"Uh, a siren?" Ezekiel skeptically clarifies. "Like not you, but a creature that sings?"

"Yes." I roll my eyes at him. "I think she will be able to hypnotize Hydra long enough for me to seize her venom."

"Sounds like a good idea." Daemon nods his approval.

I turn around and open up a portal to the faery realm. As soon as I walk through, I am greeted by a beautiful lake and the most amazing acapella you have ever heard.

"Siren?" a beautiful voice sings.

"Melody." I hug her. "It's been too long."

"What brings you our way?" Her smile drops immediately into a scowl. "I heard you were dead."

"That would be why I need your help. You see, Vulcan poisoned me with basilisk poison." She gasps. "I am okay now..."

"How?" She interrupts me, but I proceed without answering her.

"We need to use you to distract Hydra..."

"Hydra?" she interrupts in disbelief.

"Her venom is more poisonous then that of the basilisk. Do you mind?"

She just nods, but her expression is void of any emotions or thought.

"Thank you!" I open up the portal again and she comes through with me.

(DAEMON)

I am able to use my powers to get us to Xavier's in a flash.

"What happened?" he gasps out upon seeing Maddy.

"She went into the water..."

"I told you to keep her out of there." He shoots daggers at Ezekiel.

"We couldn't stop her." Ezekiel snaps defensively.

"No good comes from that place." He looks at Maddy with a thoughtful look as he takes her from Daemon and sets her on his couch. He touches her face delicately. "I have never looked at her before." Everything about his mannerisms show how much he cherishes her. He cherishes a gorgon. No, he cherishes sweet little Maddy. I can't help but smile.

"What are you smiling about?" Xavier hisses menacingly. "She could die." He chokes on the last word. I don't want Maddy to die either.

"You care for her." It's not a question, it's clear in the way he looks at her and touches her.

"Of course I do." He says softly as he looks back at her. "How is the blue haired girl?"

"She is well, as powerful as always." He smiles at me.

"You care for her." He parrots.

"Of course I do." I reply. "I really screwed things up with her." A sense of foreboding hits me. I doubt she will forgive me for my actions.

"Does she know you love her?" At this, Ezekiel perks up and looks questioningly at me.

"No." I sigh. "I'm an idiot."

"I could have told you that." Ezekiel pats me on the back and I glare at him. "We should be getting back to meet Siren."

"Yeah. Take care of Maddy." I look sternly at Xavier who gives a slight nod back. We rush back to the meeting place.

Upon returning, we see Siren and a woman with curly red hair and alabaster skin that is as fair as Siren's. Ezekiel makes a weird sound from beside me.

"This is Melody, Ezekiel and Daemon. Now that we all know each other shall we go back?" Siren asks emphatically.

"Open the way." Melody sighs.

WE GET TO THE PLACE where Hydra is, and all of us but Melody run toward the water. Melody takes a second to gauge her surroundings before following us. We get to the river and like before, all we see is water.

"Do you think she'll show up?" Siren questions.

"I don't know, but if we wait here, I'm sure she will come back eventually." I reply. It's really the only reasonable thing I could think of.

Luckily, we don't have to wait long. I see something in the water and a quick glance around, tells me they all see it too. We get into a defensive stance and Hydra springs from the water. She lunges toward us, but before she can strike, I hear the most beautiful voice.

Melody is singing and Hydra seems mesmerized, as does Ezekiel actually. Siren pounces onto the sea serpent -if serpent is what you want to call her- and a larger than normal vial appears in her hand. She takes the vial and puts it to one of the fangs of the beast.

Siren starts milking the venom like a pro and I don't think I want to know how she has become so knowledgeable. As I watch her, I am again reminded how strong, powerful and fearless she is. She fought Gwendolyn like nothing once she had her power back. The fight lasted maybe five minutes, if you include the dialogue, and Siren ended it with a simple strike. To think that I was worried about her safety as if she couldn't handle herself. Now I might have lost the one girl who I truly love.

Before long, she is jumping back down with a huge unnerving grin on her face. "Let's get back to Vulcan." Fearless and powerful

Siren opens up a portal to her home land and we are in the forest I recognize. "Why didn't you bring us right to the castle?" I question.

"We need to come up with a strategy of attack before we rush in." She nods toward a familiar cave.

"You sure you want to sleep there again?" The last time she froze.

"I'll be fine." Before anyone can continue we hear crashing in the bushes.

"What is that?" Ezekiel puts his hand on the hilt of this sword.

"A cyclops." I answer before Siren does. He draws his sword.

Siren gasps. "What are you doing?"

"Protecting us?"

She laughs at that. "Why? They're harmless."

"That thing sounds like it wants to eat our bones." He exclaims.

"They always sounds like that." She waves it off. "Let's just get in the cave."

The angry sound comes closer and through the trees I hear "Siren?" just before Stewart appears.

Siren smiles up at him, the kind of glorious smile I wish I saw more often, and preferably at me. "Stewart!" she runs over to him.

"You look better than the last time I saw you." He points at her complexion.

"Yeah, Vulcan poisoned me and now I'm here for my revenge." She joyfully states as if she is talking about going to an amusement park.

"Someone needs to take that faery down a peg... or ten." He mumbles the last part.

"I have Hydras venom." She pats her pocket, which I know is not where the vile is. I know she used her magic to safe guard it.

"Hydra?" Stewart raises a brow at us.

"Yep, she exists." Siren says cheerfully.

"Well good luck with that. Let me know if you need any help. I know some people who would love to get their hands on him." The cyclops smiles eerily.

"Will do. Well, hopefully I'll see you again soon." Siren points at the cave, "If you need us, we'll be there until the deed is done."

With that, Stewart makes his way to where ever he was going.

"So... that's a cyclops?" Ezekiel sounds confused.

"Yes." Siren smirks.

"I thought they were more fierce and vicious." He still sounds like he's trying to find his bearings.

"That's a common misconception. Now let's get in the cave so we can decide our next move."

Chapter Twenty One

(Siren)

As we sit in the cave we talk, we talk about strategy and then we talk about ourselves. It turns out that Ezekiel has been sabotaging Daemon's destruction for a very long time. In fact, 'a very long time' is vastly understating things. After all this time though, he never killed him. Maybe Daemon keeps him occupied and on his toes. Who knows the inner workings of the male psyche. It doesn't matter their species, background, life style or even the damn realm they are from, their mind is essentially the same.

I notice as we talk, that Ezekiel keeps watching Melody with longing before shaking it off and scowling at her. I wonder what that's about. Another bizarre male phenomenon. I look over to catch Daemon staring at me with the same longing I just saw on Ezekiel's face, only fiercer. As I peer into his brown eyes, they soften and then become regretful before he turns away. As I remember the terrible things he said to me before I was kidnapped, I feel a heaviness inside of me.

To know that he could walk away from me and still look at me like that is almost gut wrenching. He went off with other women, risked breaking my heart and did it anyway. All the while desiring me. I think we should really dissect and study the male brain to see how it works, or if it does at all. I take a deep breath to tamp down the hurt that has suddenly struck me.

I don't know when it happened, but I did fall for this insatiable demon who has a heart of tarnished gold. To see him look at me the way he was, makes me feel both hopeful and angry.

Hopeful because when you care about someone you want them to feel the same. Angry because he hurt me and it was all for nothing. He betrayed those words he said about only wanting me. Now that I can actually focus on living, and have the vile that will take down Vulcan, I can focus on my own heartache.

I am no longer paying attention to the chatter around me, drowning out everything but Daemon who is staring at me again almost as if he has done the same thing and I am frozen in his gaze. Then I remember, before he walked away with another female, he said I should die. I look away, feeling the hurt the memory has caused.

"I think I'm going to go outside for a bit. There is a small lake nearby and I need to wash up. I can't be too smelly for my fiancé." I finish with a hard edge and I see something dark cross Daemons face in the corner of my eye as I get up and leave the cave. I need to get away and breathe so I can remind myself why I can't allow myself to keep falling for him.

It doesn't take me long to get to the water since it's not very far away from the cave, which is something I hope neither male becomes too privy to until I am done.

I strip down to my undergarment and I am just about in the water when I hear Daemon say from behind me "You can't escape me that easily." The end of his sentence comes out in something close to what a prepubescent boy would squeak out.

I turn around and he is eyeing me up and down so slowly I can almost feel the caress of his gaze. His eyes are heated, the red ring seemingly more prominent. He says something so low I can barely make out the word but it sounds very much like "beautiful".

It takes a moment for his eyes to meet mine. "I want you Siren." He stares me down as he slowly steps toward me. "The idea of not having you is painful."

"So I can be another notch on your bedpost?" I spit. His eyes becomes wary as he continued his advance.

"That is not why." He shoots back defensively. Before I can protest he is right in front of me, hand in my hair pulling my face to his. His lips on mine are urgent and desperate as his other hand wraps around my lower back pulling me even closer. As I am pulled against his body he groans into my mouth. I mould against him perfectly and can't help but kiss him back.

"I feel like I have waited forever for this." He mumbles against my lips before he takes my mouth like a man possessed.

I finally gather my wits about me and push him away from me. "I am not someone you can come to anytime you see fit." I hiss at him. The look on his face goes from impassioned to hurt. "Once we are finished here, you can go back to Hell and find some succubus to see to your needs." I go to storm off, no longer caring if I smell from my days of not bathing until he speaks.

"I didn't have sex with any of them."

I slowly turn around with a quirked brow. "Liar." I mumble.

"I couldn't do it." He sighs. "I couldn't stop seeing your face." He is staring at the ground as if studying it before looking back up at me. "None of them were you."

"No shit." I roll my eyes and turn around to continue with my 'storming away'.

"I don't want anyone but you." I barely hear the words, but they stop me in my tracks. "I was wrong."

At that I spin on my heels angrily. "Wrong?"

"Yes, I thought you would end up being another thing for me to lose. After seeing what my father did to you, it only validated my belief." He takes a step toward me before thinking better of it. "After seeing what you did to Gwendolyn, a fierce warrior with no empathy, well, I know you are strong enough to be by my side."

I want to run over and hug him, but something gives me pause. "Strong enough to be by your side?" I spit at him. "Who do you think you are?"

"I don't ever want to put you in danger because of how I feel about you." He shouts. "I can't stand the thought of losing you forever." He chokes up.

"But you said I would be better off dead." I all but snarl.

"I love you Siren." Comes out of his mouth and I slowly turn to look at him. The look on his face tells me that he can't believe he said it either.

"What did you say?" I walk closer to him now and he watches my advance.

"You heard me." He retorts harshly.

"Aren't you afraid that I'll destroy you?" I can't help but ask.

"Can't you see? You already have." He fills the couple of steps between us and runs the back of his hand down my cheek and I close my eyes at the contact. "I haven't been the same since we met. You have destroyed me." I open my eyes to look into his which soften. "I was told I would meet a woman who would do just that, they never said that my destruction would be death. You killed the darkness in me that only lived to possess and to kill. You destroyed that part of myself that I hated the most."

"Whoa, that was deep." I smile up at him and he takes the tilt of my head as an invitation and kisses me gently. I wrap my arms around his neck and hold him to me. The kiss turns into something feral and we are ripping off each other's clothes. He has far more to take off I will admit. I don't even realize that I am at his mercy with complete abandon as he backs me up until my back hits something solid which I know has to be a tree. The trees are old with a wide girth which is perfect for what he has planned.

Without removing his mouth from mine he grabs my thigh, ordering me to raise it and open up for him. Before I can respond he is thrusting inside me all the way to the hilt. I rest my head against the tree and he kisses my exposed neck, sucking and nipping but otherwise keeping his hips still. He makes a low growling sound while pulling himself from my body only to thrust back into it with force. He is rough as he devours my body and yet through his movements I feel cherished.

I feel the most intense pleasure I have ever felt as he groans into my neck, giving me a small nip. We stay like that for a moment as I slowly lower my leg. We try to catch our breath and I feel him smile into the crook of my neck.

"Don't get cocky now." I laugh and can feel his body shake with laughter of his own as he whispers "cocky". I smile and internally shake my head.

WE WALK BACK TO THE cave where there is a weird tension between Melody and Ezekiel, although Melody gives me a wry smile and the thumbs up. I look at Daemon who puffs out his chest and puts his arm around me, pulling me snug against him.

"You're pretty dry for bathing." Melody points out mockingly.

"I don't want any details." Ezekiel looks sharply at Melody. There is a lot of weirdness going on in this cave.

Chapter Twenty Two

(Siren)

"How do I look?" I ask them after I get myself ready for my grand murder.

"Still Beautiful." Daemon replies. "Mind you it's not so much your outer appearance as much as your essence." He smiles sheepishly. "That's what drew me to you in the first place you know, your magnificent soul. I had never seen anything like it before."

"Of course." Ezekiel says with an eye roll. "That actually explains a lot."

"What?" I'm confused.

"Demons absorb beautiful souls for strength." Ezekiel answers.

"You were going to absorb my soul?" I gasp.

"You really do look different." Daemon immediately changes the subject. I don't know how I feel about this. "The frizzy light brown hair in a loose bun and dull blue eyes are going to assure you don't stand out too much. If only you could change your essence.

I close my eyes and focus on disguising any energy that I might put out into the world. "How did you do that?" He says in wonder. Ezekiel looks shocked as well.

"Whoa, that garden must have given me more mojo then I thought."

"You're all but invisible." Daemon says. "Wait, can you become invisible?"

Melody is the one to speak. "No, it's risky using any kind of magic for deceit when you live in a world where everyone uses magic. There's always the chance someone will see through it."

"No one will see through this disguise will they?" Worry etches Daemon's face.

"No one will think twice about her." Melody says with a wave of her hand.

"Now we just have to get into the castle." I grin.

AS IT TURNS OUT, GETTING into the castle was easy as pie. I have no idea how to make pie, so I can safely say that it's easier. I just walked right in and no one so much as batted an eye in my direction. Luckily I know my way around this place so there was no wandering the halls while looking lost. It doesn't take me long to make it to Vulcan's office door. I am almost positive that this is where I am going to be able to find the faerie king.

Wine materializes in my hand before I knock on the door. "Come in." comes from the other side of the door. How trusting of him. I walk into the room, void of personal belongings, but Vulcan doesn't look up. I walk over to his desk and pour him a glass of wine. "Thank you." he mumbles, but again, doesn't look up at me. I wonder if I even needed a disguise. I leave the room so he can drink up in private. I don't need to see the show, I just want to skip to the grand finale.

TWENTY-FIVE MINUTES of wandering the halls later, I go back into his office. His glass is empty and so is about a quarter of the bottle. Not a lot, but definitely enough. He still doesn't look up at me, but he's sweaty. Really sweaty. His hands are shaking a little too.

"Are you alright King Vulcan?" I wonder if he will admit to feeling a little under the weather.

"Yeah, I'm fine." He replies, still looking at whatever he's doing. Guess not. He starts coughing and is soon gasping for air in between coughs.

"Are you sure you're 'fine'? You look a little under the weather." I smile. "Look at me." I say as I slap my hand against the desk in front of him. I see his eyes look up at me. My smile widens.

"What did you put in that?" He chokes out, his voice raspy. Is he panting?

"Sorry, speak up." I pick up the bottle of wine. "I actually have no idea how Hydra's venom is going to react to your insides." I make a show of studying the bottle as if I am looking to see the venom inside.

"Hydra? She isn't real." His voice is awful quiet.

"It's funny though." I continue as if he didn't say a damn thing. "There was no warning label so I guess we'll find out the side effects together." I slowly let my true form show and his eyes bulge out of his head.

"Siren!" He gasps out in shock. "But how?"

"It doesn't matter, you won't be getting so lucky." I sit on the side of the desk to taunt him. If looks could kill...

"Cat got your tongue?" I laugh without humour. He tries to talk but he coughs. This time with blood splattering out of his mouth. Oh, this is going to be a nasty death. How exciting.

When he looks up I see blood coming out of his nose. "What did you do to me?" He seethes. It didn't sound as harsh as he intended because of his lack of energy and possible internal bleeding.

"I told you. I have no idea what will happen. Should I take notes? I feel like I should be taking notes. Oh well. I guess I'll have to replay the details in my head to make sure I remember them." I chuckle.

I pull up a chair to the front of his desk. I rest my head in my hands and watch closely. He moves his hand to punch me, but it falls onto the desk with a loud bang.

"Ouch, that must have hurt." I observe, still watching intently. "I think a little blood is coming from your ears." I turn my head to indicate taking a better look.

"You bitc..." He gets cut off by some more coughing. "I hope you rot in hell." His words are beginning to slur together making it harder for me to understand their vulgarity. It also makes me wonder what's happening to his brain. I hope it's melting.

"Is it painful?" I search his gaze for the answer and his glare darkens. "Please tell me it's painful."

"I wish you died." His words come out on a slurred whisper.

"Well obviously silly. You don't poison someone so they live a more fulfilled life." I hit the desk again. "How did it feel having my magic ripped away from you?"

"I didn't even notice." He sniffs.

"Oh Vulcan, don't cry." I say condescendingly.

"I'm not." He wipes his eyes and stares in horror at the blood on his hand.

"I can assure you that every orifice in your face is bleeding. I wonder about the other ones." I look down pointedly at his lower body. He begins to scream in agony, hunching over as he holds his stomach.

He starts vomiting blood all over the floor. As he does I notice his capillaries are bursting, leaving red trails all over his face and neck. His veins bulge before popping. Ewww, I turn away in disgust. Maybe I went a little too far with this venom, but then I remember the basilisk poison and I don't feel so bad.

Finally he collapses onto the floor, wheezing whistling breaths. I walk over to him.

"Be thankful it's a quick death, much better than the one you laid upon me." I see regret in his eyes. I kneel down beside him.

"I'm sorry." The words come out on a gust of exhalation.

"Me too Vulcan, me too." I stand up and watch my childhood friend as he takes his last breath. I stand there and think about all the times we laughed and played as children. How at one point we genuinely loved each other. All those beautiful moments that lead to this bitter one. I take a deep breath as I feel the storm of emotion inside. A tear escapes, but I quickly wipe it away. I turn around and walk out of his office. I manage to keep it together as I leave the kingdom, letting the floodgates open once outside the palace gates.

"Siren, are you hurt?" Daemon runs to me, wrapping his arms around me.

"I didn't think it would be so hard to watch him die." I sob.

"Shhh, it's done now." He tries to soothe me. "He would have only come after you until you were dead."

"I loved him once." I cry harder.

He tenses for a moment before relaxing and holding me tighter. "You will always have the memories of who he used to be, but he wasn't that person anymore." Daemon murmurs into my hair.

"I know, but it doesn't make it any easier." My tears are soaking his shirt. He just holds me and lets me cry it all out. Ezekiel and Melody look at me grimly, but the look they give each other is scathing.

We end up going back to my house in the mortal world for a celebration party. Daemon said he wanted to celebrate my life and my health. He didn't mention the death of Vulcan, but I suspect he wanted to celebrate that as well. He hasn't kept his hands off me which I enjoy immensely.

I never thought that having him would make me feel like I finally found a home, a place where I belong. I smile up at him as he kisses me gently yet thoroughly. I never thought I would fall in love with a demon. Especially this demon.

Epilogue

(Daemon)

Curse or no curse, I am incredibly happy. I still own the demon club, but mostly to insert my power over the others so they don't go rogue. I am still in charge here and I will make sure they know it. I might feel things like compassion and guilt, but they don't need to know that. Siren definitely and very efficiently obliterated me, just like it was predicted. Destruction isn't always death, and can sometimes give you the opportunity to rebuild and be made whole. Siren has definitely don't that.

With her by my side, the other demons don't question me. They obey, and for the most part, even behave. They fear her you see. When you see a little woman rip out a big scary demons heart and transform him into a blubbering baby, you tend to be a little more heedful around her. I myself am proud to be by her side. I finally got into her pants and into her heart.

She is back to volunteering at the homeless shelter which I never understood before. Now I see the joy she puts in the lives of others and how helping them lifts her spirits.

I am currently watching outside the shelter as an older man beams up at her at something she said to him. Even in her human form her smile holds my heart captive as I continue to observe her. She touches the man's arm which always makes me feel that demonic possessiveness, and then I see tendrils of magic transfer to the man. His yellowing skin gains a pink warm glow.

The woman is a mystery and one that I am lucky enough to get a lifetime to solve. As if she senses my stare she turns to me and her smile only brightens. She walks over to me and wraps her arms around me, giving me a chaste kiss that I can admittedly feel to my toes.

"Are you here to help?" she whispers.

"Actually m'lady." I give her an overdramatic bow. "I am here to take you out to dinner."

"Aren't you looking all elegant." she eyes me up and I see a mischievous look in her eyes. "Looks like I am going to have to duck out early." She yells to the back and Doris smiles while giving her the shooing motions through the window of the kitchen.

"Have fun kids." She yells to us as we walk out the door.

SIREN MANAGED TO MATERIALIZE a beautiful sheer ice blue, tight fitting dress that goes down to her knee. I'm not the only one who can't keep my eyes off her, and I am hoping that I won't have to massacre the whole damn restaurant. Her dress goes well with my navy blue suit.

The restaurant is upscale, especially for our little town. The walls are dark red with paintings on them, the linen matches the wall. There is more cutlery then I know what to do with, literally, but I thought it was the perfect place to take her after our first month of living together.

Tonight she looks like she could be a super model with her glistening blonde hair and perfect skin. Her perfection still somehow hides the creature that lurks behind the façade.

Even though the thought of losing her is an almost tangible thing, especially when I recall what it was like to see her torn apart so brutally, I also have to bear in mind that with her power, she is greater than most of the beings I have met in my lifetime. That includes my father. He would probably never guess that under this beauty, lies the faerie he almost brutally murdered.

Should that day arise, I will stand by her side fighting, because even though she will likely not need my help, and may even see it as some sort of hindrance, I will never allow her to have to fight any battle alone.

When we go back home, to our new house outside of town where our neighbours are few and far between, her human form evaporates and the faerie is revealed.

"Thank you for the lovely dinner." She purrs, as she slowly takes off her dress. Sometimes I can't believe I won her over. All it took was a few life and death situations and BAM, I had her. I rush to take off my clothes because, I'm not as seductive as she is and far less patient.

Once we make it to the bedroom, we make love to one another slowly, taking our time to revel in the moment.

I never thought I would be the kind of man to be able to do slow and gentle but with her, I find it not only more pleasurable, but also a necessity. A reminder that no matter how strong and powerful we are, we still need to feel cherished and loved which is something I feel from her every day we have been together and something I long to make her feel for the rest of our days.

Don't miss out!

Visit the website below and you can sign up to receive emails whenever Stephanie R. Lowell publishes a new book. There's no charge and no obligation.

https://books2read.com/r/B-A-XIRQ-LVSIG

Did you love *Stalked By A Demon*? Then you should read *Fell For A Gorgon*[1] by Stephanie R. Lowell!

[2]

After her friend Siren finds the underworld, Maddy finds out that the one person who might be able to cure her of her gorgon curse is a goddess who is trapped there as a punishment of her own, along with all of the other gods and goddesses.Now that Maddy knows how to get to the Underworld, she is determined to hunt this goddess down, only to find that not only will she not help her, but there is another foe who wants to get rid of the gorgon because she she has won the heart of the fallen angel Xavier, only she has no idea how he feels.

Xavier is in love with Maddy and will chase her across the Underworld if he has has to, which is exactly what he does when he

1. https://books2read.com/u/bpgYP6

2. https://books2read.com/u/bpgYP6

runs into his old friend Delilah who tells him that Maddy has been imprisoned and has met her fate.

When things get heated in prison, her curse is lifted and now she has to adjust to a new kind of life where she is finally beautiful, only now Xavier has to prove that he loved her all along, even when she was a gorgon, all while trying to keep her safe from the jealous goddess.

Also by Stephanie R. Lowell

Caught with a Lycan
Caught in a Lycan Favour
Caught in a Lycan's Protection
Caught Vamping Around With A Lycan
Caught Bewitching a Lycan

Love at first bite
The Vampire's Obsession

Lovers Of Lore
Stalked By A Demon
Fell For A Gorgon

The Moonstone Trilogy
The Druid Descendant
The Nephilim Rises
The Return Of Satan

Standalone

The Dimension to Destiny

About the Author

Stephanie R. Lowell has enjoyed writing for as long as she can remember. She used to write poetry and songs before getting into novels. She has always had a strong imagination and is thankful that adulthood hasn't stolen that away completely.

Stephanie loves making other's laugh and truly believes that it's the key to longevity.

www.ingramcontent.com/pod-product-compliance
Lightning Source LLC
Jackson TN
JSHW022045240725
88250JS00001B/12
* 9 7 9 8 2 3 1 0 0 1 0 3 3 *